ALSO BY

Gristle & Bone (collection)

Salvage (novella)

Wildfire (novella)

Woom (novella)

Where the Monsters Live (novella)

The Method (novel)

Video Nasties (collection)

Ebenezer (novella)

Ghostland (novel)

The Midwives (novel)

IN EVERY DARK CORNER

HORROR STORIES

DUNCAN RALSTON

SHADOW WORK PUBLISHING

COPYRIGHT

For Rex Garrote,
who inspired me more than he will ever know.

INTRODUCTION

You just have to trust in your own madness.

CLIVE BARKER

Welcome.

If this is your first foray into my admittedly twisted mind, it's not too late to turn around. Some of the stories contained within this book may shock or disgust you. Don't claim you haven't been warned.

Aside from the screenplay at the end of this book, the stories you'll find in my third collection of dark fiction have been published elsewhere but have never been collected in a single volume. One of them—*Where the Monsters Live*—has never been printed in its current form.

Because the stories are so vastly different in tone and content, I'm going to be doing something a little different this time around. Each story will have notes at the end explaining a bit of the thought process behind them. A bit of the *madness*, if you will.

When you have a story about a sentient penis and another about religious zealots torturing an atheist on Christmas running head to head—so to speak—it's probably a good idea to explain why they may or may not belong in the same book together.

The real reason I've collected them is that none of them has really gotten the exposure—again, so to speak—as some of my more popular stories from *Gristle & Bone* and *Video Nasties*. And... I happen to *like* these stories. They're fun and dark and disturbing. I hope you have as much fun reading them as much as I did writing them.

Until we meet again, keep it creepy.

HEAD

Traeger tipped the driver and stepped out of the running courtesy car. He slung his overnight bag onto his shoulder to avoid eye contact as he passed a pair of Hare Krishnas offering their limp colorful flowers for a handful of change, and lugged the bowling bag to the airport doors. Lighting his last Chesterfield—Bogart's brand of choice—he took a drag as the building's air conditioning began to cool his face. The Big Apple in August was hot enough to fill a pie and Traeger welcomed the luxury.

Traffic had been murder and he was already running a bit late. He sidestepped a bank of life insurance kiosks inside but stopped briefly to pick up another package of Chesterfields from the cigarette machine for the flight. When he reached his gate, passengers had already begun boarding. The plane departed in twenty minutes.

Trips like this were typical in Traeger's line of work: a quick job, an overnight stay in some fleabag airport hotel with a coin-operated bed, jet back home in the morning. Often—like today—he would return with a souvenir in his overnight bag. He'd never check the bag, would always carry it onboard. After the latest unaccompanied suitcase bombings, Traeger suspected baggage handlers would be checking for explosives without permission.

Nobody ever gave him trouble at the gate, and he expected today to be no different. Still, it was a big risk, what he had in the bowling bag. Far riskier than the usual drugs, money or stolen items. How could he possibly explain the severed head of a notorious union boss, mummy-wrapped in tea towels and packing tape where the bowling ball should be?

The agent took his ticket and Traeger flashed his best I'm-a-normal-businessman's smile. He was still sweating from the drive over. He felt it on his brow and under his arms—he was practically swimming in his underpants. The AC unit in his hotel room had been on the fritz and the moment he'd stepped out of the shower he'd accumulated a fresh layer of perspiration. Under normal circumstances conspicuous sweating might draw suspicion. August in New York in the midst of a heatwave and even the ticket agent had noticeable stains under the arms of her blouse.

She returned his smile and ticket, gave his bags a quick, dismissive look and ushered him through.

As he descended the escalator to the runways a couple of air marshals stepped in from below. Heat from the tarmac blew in behind them like air from a cheap hotel hair dryer. His pulse, normally as perfectly timed as a Buddy Rich drum riff, suffered a momentary blip as their paths crossed. They returned the nod he offered.

A sweaty gym sock of muggy heat slapped him in the face when he stepped outside. Christ, he was glad to be getting out of this toxic waste dump of a city! The DC-10 pilot greeted a few stragglers climbing the stairs, mostly men in tweed or plaid suit jackets and pleated pants. A couple of black men loaded the remaining few pieces of luggage into the cargo hold, laughing and making easy jive talk. Elsewhere, mechanics worked on the underside of a 727. The buzz of an air wrench gave way to the shriek of a jet engine, and Traeger shaded his eyes against the sun to look out at the runway.

A big Concorde had reached takeoff speed and its tapered nose lifted off the ground.

Traeger blew an impressed whistle. He'd been fascinated by air travel since he was about six or seven. Gigantic hunks of metal hurtling themselves into the air, defying the laws of nature.

Back then, he'd been partial to Fokkers and Japanese Zeroes, the Supermarine Spitfire. These days it was the Concorde, for its impressive speed and sleek body. He hadn't had the opportunity to fly on one yet but one day he wanted to take the supersonic flight from New York to London. His job allowed no time for it, so it remained a retirement goal.

Unfortunately, retirement was looking less and less likely. These days hungry young kids willing to do the job for peanuts gobbled up all the smaller jobs that had kept Traeger afloat between larger paydays like this one. The Company trusted him with high-profile gigs now but how long would that last into his twilight years? Who would trust a contractor who dribbled while tying his sneakers?

Traeger dropped his cigarette on the tarmac among several discarded butts from other passengers and crushed it under the sole of a tassel loafer. Either the heat or the nicotine was starting to make him feel loopy. His sweat-slick palms slipped on the handrail as he pulled himself eagerly up the airstairs.

The pilot welcomed him and nodded toward the bowling bag. "What do you bowl? Ten-pin or five?"

Traeger sputtered. He didn't bowl at all but the pretense was important. "I haven't bowled five-pin since my eighth birthday, Cap."

"Good man," the pilot said. He snapped Traeger a salute. "Welcome aboard."

Traeger slipped into the cool, recycled atmosphere of the aircraft. Stewardesses were already slipping meal trays onto a cart. He winked at the busty older redhead. He would have preferred joining the Mile-High Club with the younger brunette but she didn't even glance in his direction. Probably for the best. Mixing business with pleasure was never wise, particularly 20,000 feet in the air.

"Could either of you lovely ladies bring me a boilermaker when you get a chance? I'm in B-15."

The brunette's eyes narrowed ever so slightly as she glanced at her partner. Even though the redhead smiled like she'd remember his order, Traeger was sure he'd have to remind her when they came around with the food.

The drink was inconsequential. What mattered again was the pretense. Act like a salesman, slightly aggressive but not disruptive. These women expected a man like him to flirt. The pilot expected small talk. Not living up to these expectations was likelier to draw suspicion.

Traeger made his way to the middle of the plane, heading down the aisle to the left. He'd asked to be seated in the aisle, close to the wing. He liked to watch the flaps lower and rise, to see the ailerons vibrate from atmospheric pressure and watch the flow of air and cloud ripple over the top of the wing. It also gave him control of the overhead compartments, where he would store his overnight bag.

The plane was mostly full. Traeger passed three men sitting in the middle seats, all dressed in similar plaid suit jackets, a style he wished had died with the '70s, along with disco and casual cocaine use. In the row behind them sat an elderly lady with an oxygen tank, and a beleaguered-looking woman who could have been her much younger twin. Her young son flew a toy airplane over the back of his seat, reminding Traeger of himself when he was a boy. He had to resist the urge to tousle the kid's hair.

He stopped and waited for a portly bald man with beady dark eyes and large features to shove a suitcase into the overheads a row up from B. The guy made him think of Alfred Hitchcock in the old TV series. Hitch twisted and turned the suitcase several times, trying to cram a circular peg in a square hole. Out of patience, Traeger grabbed the bag and managed to fit it in lengthwise.

"Thanks," Hitch said, giving Traeger a brief once-over.

"No problem."

The man wedged into his row and began the process again, trying to fit his girthy hips into the narrow seat. Traeger moved on indifferently. He opened the overhead above his seat, found it empty but for a brown leather duffel and slipped his overnight bag in alongside it.

He sat down beside a black man in a three-piece suit, the jacket folded over his lap. The man looked up from an inflight magazine and smiled as Traeger tucked the bowling bag between his knees.

"No room in the overheads?" the man asked.

"Huh?"

The man gestured toward Traeger's bag.

"Oh. It's my medications."

"Yeah? I'm a diabetic. Got to prick my finger every few hours, check my glucose levels. Pain in my ass."

"You'd think it'd be a pain in your finger."

The man chuckled. Stuck out a hand. "Name's Voss. Henry Voss."

Traeger eyed the hand a moment, looking for pricks— reluctant to become accidental blood brothers with a stranger. He shook it. "Dennis Traeger."

"Good to meet you, Dennis Traeger. What business are you in, you don't mind me asking?"

"Insurance," Traeger replied, his go-to for derailing casual conversation. "Life, mostly. Some incidentals."

"You don't say." Henry Voss suddenly seemed very eager to return to the magazine. He pointed to a full-page ad, a well-dressed white couple in luxuriant, roomy airplane seats. The woman had a portable computer on the tabletop and the man seemed to be dictating to her while an attractive stewardess served champagne. The caption said *Welcome to the New Business Class.* "Is she supposed to be his wife or his secretary, you think?" Voss asked.

Traeger chuckled. "Does that look like the face of a guy who's getting laid? Gotta be his wife."

Voss laughed. Traeger lit a cigarette. He offered the pack to Voss, who shook his head.

"I quit. Doctor said it was bad for me, 'cause of the diabetes. You believe that?"

"The wonders of modern medicine." Traeger exhaled a fragrant cloud. "Christ, I don't know what I'd do if I couldn't smoke!"

"Calms the nerves," Voss said with a nod. "You know, Rod Serling smoked Chesterfields."

"Rod Serling? The actor?"

Voss smiled patiently, shaking his head. "You know the show *Twilight Zone*." He sang the theme, "Neener neener, neener neener."

"I'm not much for sci-fi. Listen, I'm gonna get some shut-eye—"

Voss held up a hand. "Say no more. I've gotta get caught up on my reading anyhow." He flipped a page to a piece about the Challenger space shuttle. "Hey, look at that. First woman in space. Only a matter of time before they put a black man up there, huh?"

"I think there's a colored—I mean a black guy—on the next launch."

"Oh yeah?" Voss smiled. "A brother in space. How about that?"

Voss returned to the article. Satisfied he would no longer be interrupted, Traeger leaned against the headrest and closed his eyes. A moment later the captain came on announcing the flight was about to take off. Five minutes later, they were in the air.

———

TRAEGER WOKE to a muddled voice whispering in his ear.

The plane hit turbulence and he jolted upright, worried about the bowling bag. It was still in his lap, still zipped. He breathed a sigh of relief and peered out he window. Dark already. He must have nodded off and slept right through dinner and drink service. His neck was stiff and he felt groggy enough to fall back to sleep.

He studied his seatmate, Voss, who lay with his head against his suit jacket pressed up against the wall and his eyes closed. Guy didn't even need a pillow, with his hairstyle—what did you call it? An Afro, that was it.

"Thought you got away with it, huh?"

Traeger startled at the voice. His seatmate's lips hadn't moved, though it was difficult to be sure in the dim light. He stared at Voss a long moment before deciding it couldn't have been him, even if the man was a trained ventriloquist. The shallow, steady breathing indicated sleep. To his left was a young couple. The guy was listening to music on a blue Walkman, staring at the back of the seat in front of him and bobbing his head. Traeger heard a vague tinny sound from the kid's goofy-looking headphones. The girl was reading a paperback copy of *Valley of the Dolls* with the overhead light on.

"Down here, asshole," the grim voice said from his lap.

Despite his better judgment, Traeger looked down. Somehow, the voice had come from between his legs—or, more accurately, from the head inside the bowling bag. From that goddamn commie union boss "Holy" Joe Hillier. From the head that had been until quite recently still attached to its body.

I'm still asleep, Traeger thought. *I'm having a nightmare.*

"*You're* having a nightmare?" Holy Joe said, his voice slightly muffled from within the leather bag. "I'm the one trapped in the dark. Smells like rental shoes and friggin' Hi Karate in here, you scum-sucking prick."

Traeger covered the bag with his jacket, looking around to see if anyone had heard. Of course, no one had. He might not have been dreaming but he was certain Hillier's voice was a product of his imagination. Which meant he'd lost his damn marbles.

"*Non compos mentis*," Hillier agreed. "You ain't just lost your marbles, pal. You lost the whole stinkin' bag!"

Traeger stood abruptly, clutching the bag to his chest in an effort to keep the mouthy head quiet. The plane shuddered again, throwing him into the seat ahead. The guy who looked like Alfred Hitchcock glanced up with a scowl from a newspaper crossword he was filling in with a fountain pen in neat capital letters. Traeger apologized hurriedly and carried on to the restrooms, hoping like hell they were unoccupied.

The redhead stewardess stood up from the jump seat as he approached the restrooms. "Sir, we're experiencing turbulence, please return to your—"

"Urgent business," he said, tearing open the restroom door. He plopped down on the toilet seat lid, pulled the door shut and locked it. "Shit, shit, shit! Get yourself together, man."

He felt himself beginning to hyperventilate, sweating again despite coolness of the aircraft's interior. He heard the stewardesses discussing him behind the door, their sibilant whispers like fighting snakes.

"Yeah, get it together," Hillier said, making Traeger jump. "Wish I could do that. But I can't, 'cause you cut off my friggin' head and dumped my stiff in the East River!"

Shrieking like a sewer rat, Traeger cast the bag onto the sink and stared at it in the mirror. "You're not real," he said.

"Oh, I'm real," Hillier said. "I'm super-duper extra-primo real, my friend. And those folks out there, they're gonna start to notice me real soon. Go on and open up the bag, you don't believe me."

Traeger eyed the sealed zipper. He wouldn't entertain the thought. If he unzipped the bag he'd be giving himself over to his delusion. That way lay madness.

But if Hillier was right, if the tape had split and the towels had slipped off... if the head started to *stink*...

Christ! He had to know.

Slowly, Traeger stood and leaned over the sink. His reflection looked ghoulish under the overhead light: long shadows hooding his sunken eyes, salt-and-pepper five-o'clock shadow on his sharp cheekbones and chin. He unzipped the bag and drew it open. The pungent smell struck him immediately and he reeled back in disgust before peering down into the dark crevasse.

Hillier's head lay in an unholy halo of soiled tea towels, torn packing tape, cauliflower ears, and shaggy, sandy-blond hair flecked with blood. His neck had been severed at a clean angle just below his stubbly double chin, a wound Traeger had cauterized with the hotel iron to prevent blood from seeping into the bag during the flight.

The corpse's eyes snapped open.

Traeger dropped the bag in horror, staggering back until his calves struck the toilet. He plopped back down on the seat, his teeth clattering together painfully.

Holy Joe spat a strip of shredded tape and said, "Told ya."

"You can't talk," Traeger said.

"Tell it to your shrink."

Traeger shook his head. "I've lost my goddamn mind."

"Not yet, you haven't."

"Shhhh!" Traeger pressed the heels of his palms against his eyes until he saw stars. "You need to shut up."

"You can't hide from your conscience, Traeger. And you can't hide me in here much longer, either. I hate to admit it, but I am *fragrant*. They're gonna catch a whiff of me soon, like a ripe gorgonzola, and when they do, you're going down for a long time, believe you me. Head in a bag? You're looking at life in prison, that's if you're lucky—"

Traeger stood. He grabbed the cannister of lemon-scented disinfectant spray from the sink.

"Hey now wait a minute, pal—"

He pressed the trigger and emptied the contents of the cannister into the bag, ozone layer be damned.

"You think that's gonna shut me up?"

But it did. Hillier began to cough and spit and after a few seconds he fell silent. Traeger peered down at the head, now glistening with a thick layer of sticky, lemon-stinking deodorizer. The eyes were shut and the mouth closed the way they had been before he'd covered the head in rags.

Had he imagined it all?

A loud knock on the door startled him. He called out, "What?" trying to sound as calm as possible and failing miserably.

"Sir, the pilot has asked that you please return to your seat immediately."

The other stewardess this time, not the redhead. She sounded beyond aggravation.

"Much as I would love to, this one's gonna be a double-flusher, I think."

He could practically hear the woman cringe behind the door. He chuckled at the thought before Hillier suddenly began shouting: *"Help! Help! This psycho chopped my head off and stuffed me in a bowling bag!"*

Traeger zipped up the bag with a startled yelp and Hillier cackled with laughter. Desperate, Traeger swung the bag over the toilet, raised the lid and peered into the bowl.

"You wouldn't dare," Hillier said, apparently able to read his mind.

"I would!" Traeger shot back. But the pipe was only a few inches in diameter, and even if he could fit Hillier's fat head through the hole, he'd be returning home without his cargo. The Company would kill him for much less. Botching a high-profile job like this, Mr. Redman might even do it himself, with his bare hands.

There was only one option. He stared at the hinged fold in the door, reluctant to go back out there with the chatterbox severed head in his bag. How long could he stand listening to the damned thing? Judging by the time on his watch there was just over three hours left until they reached LAX. Three hours. Christ.

"Maybe you'll get the chair," Hillier suggested. "I guess it depends which state they arrest you in, huh? Hey, that reminds me of an old joke: if a plane crashes on the border between the U.S. and Canada, where do they bury the survivors?"

Ignoring him, Traeger kicked off his right loafer and slipped off the sock. Before Hillier could protest he crammed the sweaty thing into the man's fat gob. Quickly, he folded the tea towels back over Hiller's eyes and mouth and did his best to salvage the packing tape, sealing it with scraps. When he was satisfied with the job he zipped up the bag, pulled the latch from Occupied red to Vacant green, and drew open the door. The brunette stewardess rose from the jump seat with her eyebrows screwed together.

"I wouldn't go in there for a bit," Traeger said, pulling the door shut behind him. The stewardess made a sour face, and Traeger turned toward face cabin. He seemed to be free and clear, for the moment. Could he make it to his seat without incriminating himself further?

"Nowhere!" came Hillier's muffled punchline. "They don't bury survivors! You geddit?"

The plane hit turbulence and Traeger braced against the wall. The stewardess returned to her seat beside her partner, giving him a look like he'd just trailed out a cloud of shit from the can while Hillier laughed uproariously. Traeger clutched the bag close to his chest. The women eyed it with suspicion.

"I still want that boilermaker," Traeger snapped. He could feel them watching as he hurried back down the aisle. Hitchcock's lookalike had stopped filling in the crossword to goggle at him. Traeger flashed the man something between a snarl and a grin and glanced at the puzzle. He startled. The man had filled the word HEAD in the horizontal and the vertical. Had Hitch seen inside the bag somehow? Could he *smell* it? Traeger couldn't be sure but he thought so.

He hurried past and opened the overhead. The plane seemed to drop a frightening distance before steadying again and he fumbled and nearly dropped the bag. His hip struck the seat in front of him and Hitch looked up again with a pouty scowl. Traeger stuffed the bowling bag—*"Don't put me in there in the dark, c'mon, be a pal!"* the head pleaded—into the bin, slammed the door closed and dropped into his seat with a sigh.

"Feeling okay?"

Traeger turned his head. Voss was eyeing him cautiously.

"I'm fine, thanks."

"Took your meds, did you?"

Who the hell did this guy think he was? "That's right," Traeger snapped.

"What's your ailment, you don't mind me asking?"

Traeger gave the man an aggrieved look. "Mister, you don't wanna know."

Voss nodded. "Okay. That's fair." He leaned back against the headrest. "You know, I'm a psychologist." He turned to Traeger with a grin. "I know what you're thinking. You're thinking the average white man'd have to be really messed up to see a black psychologist. But the people I see don't have much of a choice. I'm a forensic psychologist. Most of my patients, if you could call them that, are either dead or in prison."

"Is that right?" Traeger said. The man's voice was calming. At least he didn't have to listen to that damned head anymore.

"Uh-huh," Voss said. "So I know the look."

Traeger turned so he was fully facing the man, intrigued. "What look is that?"

"The look of a man walking a tightrope between sanity and the abyss."

Above their heads, Hillier began to titter.

Traeger wiped sweat off his brow, fighting the urge to look up.

"*He knows—hee-hee-hee... he knows, he knows he knows...*"

"What are you on? Antidepressants? Barbiturates? Haloperidol?"

Traeger hadn't heard the question. He nodded, swallowing hard.

"Well, which one?"

"The uh, the last thing."

"Haldol." Voss nodded thoughtfully. "You must be going through hell right about now. Is it voices? Are they telling you to do things, Dennis?"

"You didn't tell him your name," Hillier whispered conspiratorially.

Didn't he? Yes. The psychologist had said his name was Voss—Something Voss—and Dennis had said 'Dennis Traeger,' like it meant nothing at all to tell a stranger his real name.

Traeger forced himself to nod.

"Are they telling you to hurt people, Dennis?"

"Yes!" the head shouted. "Hurt people! Rape the stewardess! Grab the pen and jab it through the crossword right into Alfie's groin!"

Traeger shook his head.

"Are they telling you to hurt yourself?"

"Slit your wrists! Open up your throat and spill your stinking guts on the shrink's lap! Take a flying fucking leap out the window, you scum-sucking prick!"

Traeger barely managed to shake his head again.

"Kill yourself! Guilty! Kill yourself kill yourself kill yourself!"

Traeger screamed and launched out of his chair. Voss's eyes opened comically wide as Traeger fumbled with the latch, tore open the overhead compartment, and grabbed the bag. Behind him the guy with the Walkman raised his headphones with a look of indifferent curiosity unique to the young. The elderly lady peered around the seatback and the kid stopped his toy airplane in mid-flight, gawping.

Traeger saw none of this. His eyes were on the bag in his hands. "Shut up!" he screamed down at it. "Shut up shut up shut up!"

Voss raised his hands, palms out. "It's okay, Dennis. The voices—they aren't real. They're just in your head."

"Head!" Traeger screamed.

That was it, the last straw. They all knew. They were all

in on it, conspiring against him with Holy Joe's head. He had to get rid of the damned thing, but where?

Traeger spotted the EXIT sign. He turned for it and ran, clutching the bag like a fullback heading for the end zone. Hillier laughed as Traeger dashed past the restrooms and stopped in front of the door. He laughed as Traeger unzipped the bag and shoved the brunette stewardess back into her seat. He laughed as Traeger grabbed the emergency handle and jerked it all the way around.

"There!" Traeger shouted. "Who's laughing now, asshole?"

Voss shouted, "Dennis, please! You don't have to do this!"

"Oh no?"

Traeger pulled the head out by the hair and held it up. The jaw had fallen open and twisted in a horrible rictus. Bloodshot green eyes stared in vacant horror at the passengers. Voss cringed. The people closest to Traeger, roused awake by the disturbance, gasped in terror. The old lady wilted into the aisle over the side of her chair and her oxygen tank rolled away from her limp body.

"Yeah," Traeger said. "Now you see."

Without another word he kicked the door open and shoved the head back in the bag. The door sucked outward with a thud and a huge rush of air and the bowling bag tore from his grip, shooting out into the cloudless night. Traeger laughed maniacally as loose newspaper pages and empty meal trays hurled passed him and out the gaping doorway.

For a moment he thought he was free—finally free—and then the atmospheric pressure grabbed him in a frigid fist and dragged him out into space.

Jet engines roaring over his head, Traeger hurtled back at a steep angle, caught for a moment in the slipstream... and then he was freefalling, watching the giant DC-10 grow smaller in the distance as the ground rose beneath him, his suit jacket billowing, hair whipping in his face.

There were worse ways to go. He could have been buried alive. He could have burned to death. He could have been eaten away by cancer or taken a shot in the gut and drowned in his own fluids. This wasn't so bad. In fact, now that he could no longer hear the engines it was almost serene.

He thought back to his youth, when he'd sat in the grass staring up at the sky as jet trails bloomed overhead and wondered what it might be like to be so far up in the air without a care in the world, sipping after-dinner cocktails like the ads he saw in magazines.

Out in the vast open darkness he heard laughter.

"No," he gasped. "No—God, no!"

He saw the bowling bag, a beige spot growing larger in the distance below his feet. It caught in the wind, opening like a parachute, and "Holy" Joe's head came tumbling out. The man was laughing.

"The head! The goddamned head!" Traeger screamed. The frigid wind stole the words from his lips, and he began to laugh himself until he cried.

Hillier's laughter followed Traeger until his body crashed to the earth. Every bone in Traeger's body crushed in a single agonizing moment, flesh, bone and organs sluicing across an open field.

When his remains were found the following morning, it was difficult to determine which head belonged with the body. The coroner placed both heads in the same bag.

NOTES: This story was originally published in Death's Head Press's *Dig Two Graves* anthology in 2019, and came to fruition when they approached me to write something for the anthology. I'd been tooling around with the concept for a while: a story about a hitman with a head in a bowling bag, but it wasn't until I started writing it that I realized it would be impossible for anyone to get on a plane with a severed head post-9/11, no matter how discretely it was packed. So I decided to do it as a period piece, setting it during a time in which E.C. Comics *Tales from the Crypt* were still very much a thing. Since I love the era and I'd always intended it to give the story an E.C. Comics feel, the decision felt like a NO-BRAINER. *Heh, heh, heh!**

*EDITOR's NOTE: *please read the preceding two sentences in the Crypt Keeper's voice.*

THE BOATS

"Most folks think what makes the Everglades dangerous is the gators, but there are plenty of other things that can kill you in these beautiful blasted wetlands, Tolland.

"Snakes, for one. Did you know a Burmese python will wrap itself around a man and crush him to death in minutes? You didn't know that, did you? I'm a student of nature, Tolland. The animal kingdom fascinates me."

Xavier Tolland kept quiet, studying the cypress trees rising from placid dark water as the boats passed them by. Their wide gray trunks reminded him of the gowns young girls wore at their cotillions, which in turn got him thinking about the first time he'd found himself in over his head for a girl.

He'd met his first beau at her debutante ball when they were both fifteen and he'd slipped under her gown to eat her raw on her father's billiard table. After she'd come she'd yanked up her panties, thrust her petticoat down and scurried back to the party without returning the favor. Worse, she'd squealed to her father who'd had Tolland forcibly ejected from the premises with his pants around his ankles.

This brief encounter had set the tone for every relationship since until Charlotte Liddell. What he and Charlotte had was special, a love so strong it had swallowed him whole.

And still he'd ended up in deep water.

"You might want to listen to this, Tolland."

Straining, Tolland raised his head to look at the wooden boat towing him. Franklin Riley Liddell reclined in the backseat while his man, a brawny brainless Greek named Aristotle, rowed. Liddell held what Tolland had mockingly called a "dueling pistol" in one limp wrist draped over a cocked knee. He wore a boater hat, the kind popularized by barbershop quartets, and kept his short-sleeved white linen shirt unbuttoned to show his deep red tan and sparse golden chest hair.

The man was a Southern dandy of the worst kind, loathed by wife, children and employees. Tolland had worked for the company founded by Liddell's grandfather, Liddell Excavation, for thirteen years. Due more to charisma than skill he'd moved quickly through the ranks from heavy equipment operator to senior manager. As a laborer Tolland had suspected his superiors didn't give a damn for him or his coworkers. As Liddell's second-in-command he'd witnessed firsthand the man's ruthless contempt was not limited solely to employees.

It was for this reason he hadn't hesitated to lay the charm on Charlotte Liddell at a company barbecue on the Liddell estate, the former Bonnie Brae plantation, and the two had made time to see each other as often as possible in the seven months since. Five years his senior, Liddell's third wife had melted in his muscular arms and come buckets under the ministrations of his calloused hands.

"I'm long passed taking orders from you, Liddell," Tolland grunted.

Liddell shrugged. "Fair enough. I suppose I should satisfy myself with your present condition."

"You'll have to satisfy yourself plenty once Charlotte finds out about this."

The dandy chuckled lightly. "Oh don't flatter yourself, Tolland. Do you honestly think you're the first man she'd slinked around with behind my back? Charlotte has very little to do all day besides spend my money. You, my dear friend, were merely a chew toy for an anxious little bitch."

Tolland clenched his jaw, stewing in impotent rage. With his head, hands and feet fixed between two wooden boats similar to the one Aristotle rowed his movement was limited. The contraption held him almost like a medieval stockade, although he lay spread eagle and facedown across the wooden seats. The boat above held him firmly in place. Liddell, or more likely Aristotle, had constructed this torture device specific to his measurements.

Obviously letting Charlotte buy him a suit had been a bad call.

A stump dragged along the bottom of the boat. As it reached the stern the bow dipped, plunging Tolland's face into brackish water up to his nose. He got a mouthful of algae and scum before he could turn his head and spit, which reminded him of Charlotte's habit of letting him come in her mouth, spitting it into a tissue and flushing it down the toilet.

Isn't that how they got all those alligators in the New York sewers? he wondered.

"Speaking of big mouths," Liddell said. "If you're lucky a gator will come along swiftly and put you out of your misery. If you're *unlucky*, and all visible evidence points to that being likely, you'll experience what Aristotle's people were unfortunate enough to endure at the hands of the ancient Persians.

"The boats, or scaphism as it's also called, was used as a brutal form of torture and execution in the centuries leading up to the Christian era. They put Mithridates to death this way. I won't bore you with lurid details as you'll soon discover them yourself. Suffice to say your death will be a long, drawn-out and painful affair, much like my relationship with Charlotte has been."

A mosquito bit Tolland on his bare ass. The weirdest part about this business with the boats had been when they'd made him strip down in front of the Hummer before marching him into the water. He'd suspected Liddell or the Greek had just wanted to see him naked, maybe for sexual reasons, maybe to find what sort of tool had been operating on his wife.

"Hey, Liddell. Why don't you open this thing up and scratch my ass for me?"

The man pooched out his lower lip in aggravation and Tolland chuckled. He truly believed you had to take pleasure in the little things if you wanted to survive in this world.

Aristotle rowed the boat onto a small hammock surrounding a gigantic mangrove choked by strangling fig. He stepped out, sinking into the black water above his hip waders, and pulled the boat ashore.

Maybe they'll quit playing games and get this beating over and done with so I can go home already.

Liddell stood, balancing himself as the boat wobbled. For a delicious moment Tolland thought the man might plunge headfirst into the swamp, but Liddell steadied himself and Tolland swallowed bitter disappointment, watching his former superior return safely to dry land.

Aristotle returned to the boat. He unhooked the towrope from the back and dragged Tolland's floating torture device along the gunwale until he was close enough to shore to step out into the shallow water. Aristotle's groin came within inches of Tolland's face, and if he got close enough, Tolland promised himself he'd bite no matter what part of him was within reach.

Eat or be eaten, he thought.

But Aristotle held the rope high, wary of Tolland's exposed limbs and teeth. He waded in up to his chest and latched the towrope on a mooring ring secured to a cypress. Then he splashed a hand beneath the water and brought up a set of keys.

The Greek unlatched the padlocks at bow and stern and raised the boat off Tolland's back. It swung on its squeaky hinges and splashed down beside its twin, rocking the boat Tolland lay in.

With the weight off his back he tried to stretch out his limbs and spine, but since they'd tied his forearms and lower legs to the seats it didn't help much. If not for the ropes he would have risked escape despite Liddell's dueling pistol and the fifty pounds of muscle Aristotle had on him. Truthfully he hadn't expected Liddell's little game to get this far. A bit naïve on his part, especially since he'd seen firsthand the extremes to which Liddell would go when a client tried to fuck him over.

He'd thought the talk of torture and scaffolding—or whatever the fuck Liddell had called it—was just playacting. That at worst they'd bring him out here, rough him up a bit, and let him walk home naked through the swamp.

The boats rotated languidly. Tolland watched Aristotle return to the rowboat and lug a large white tub out of the back. It splashed down heavily into the water. Aristotle floated it to the boats by its handle.

Tolland noticed the cartoon bee on its label. Below were the words RAW HONEY.

Aristotle peeled off the lid and set it inside the boat. He reached into the tub, scooped out a handful of thick golden honey and began to smear it over Tolland's left arm.

"What the fuck is this, Liddell?"

The dandy chuckled. "As my lovely wife might have told you, Tolland, you attract more flies with honey than with vinegar."

Aristotle slathered the sticky honey over Tolland's shoulder blades and down his back. When his ass cheeks were coated the man cupped his balls and stabbed a thick finger into Tolland's asshole like he was giving him a veterinary exam. Tolland squealed in horror, trying to squirm away. Both Liddell and Aristotle laughed.

"He's a shy one, isn't he?" Liddell said.

Aristotle slopped his hand into the tub and slapped more honey onto Tolland's legs. He came back with the bucket and smeared gooey globs in Tolland's hair, over his face, and into his mouth.

Tolland spat the sickly sweet substance back at Aristotle but the man ignored the thick goober, snapped the lid on and returned it to the rowboat. He came back to Tolland with the padlock keys between his straight white teeth, waded around the stern and began raising the other from the water.

"No!" Tolland shouted, struggling against the ropes. "No, you can't do this, Liddell!"

"Oh but I can!" Liddell said as the boat slammed down hard on Tolland's back, a gasped breath exploding from Tolland's lungs. Aristotle snapped the padlocks into place while Tolland caught his breath and waded back to the hammock.

"I'll let you in on a little secret, Tolland." Liddell swatted a fly on his neck and flicked it away in distaste. "My Charlotte has had many affairs before you barked up her tree. She didn't fall apart when any of those men disappeared. And the woman truly is a creature of habit."

"You're wrong, Liddell. Charlotte and I love each other."

Liddell smiled amusedly. "I wish I could be here when you realize how wrong you are. Alas..." He made a sweeping gesture toward the rowboat. "I have a business to run, and Liddell Excavation is going to need a new senior manager."

Liddell returned to his boat and sat in the back. Aristotle pushed it from shore and jumped in soaking wet. His employer cringed away from him.

"Dammit, Ari! You're dripping on my trousers."

Without a word of apology Aristotle picked up the oars and began to row them away. As they passed, Liddell lazily raised a hand in farewell. "Ta-ta, Tolland. You treacherous snake."

"I'm gonna kill you, Liddell. I'm gonna get out of this fucking thing and I'm gonna tear your goddamn head off!"

"I very much doubt that."

Tolland couldn't see the man anymore but Liddell's tone had a smirking quality to it.

The sound of the oars splashing into the water and scraping the gunwale diminished until they were gone, and the only sounds were the creaks and groans of the trees, and the canopy swishing in a light summer wind.

He truly was alone.

The thought made him shiver despite the muggy heat inside the boats. Loneliness was one thing he could never abide. Since his mother abandoned him in his early teens he'd moved from one relationship to the next the way a roofer lay shingles. Women offered him temporary comfort. He'd thought his affair with Charlotte would be different, and yesterday he would have happily believed they might run away and grow old together. Now he knew it was a fool's fantasy. As much as she'd professed her love to him she never would have left her husband's money behind. Short of robbing Liddell blind Tolland would have had to be content with fucking another man's wife for the rest of his life, or at least until she'd grown tired of him and moved on.

Chew toy, Tolland thought bitterly. Was that really all she'd thought of him? Or was Liddell just kidding himself?

His joints ached, the limbs prickled with numbness. Pressed against divots carved into the gunwale his wrists, ankles and throat felt bruised. Gnats had swarmed around his head, green bottle flies and houseflies landed in his hair and whined in his ears and he couldn't swat them away. Mosquitoes and horseflies stung his neck and hands, his skin burned from the hot summer sun and starting to peel.

The boats thudded up against the cypress and scraped along its rough hide. Tolland grasped a chunk of protruding bark and held them still, hoping to gauge the lay of the land.

The hammock created by the roots of the mangrove and years of clotted gray muck lay maybe fifteen feet from what he'd come to think of as "his tree." Much too far to reach while trapped within the boats. Everywhere else was water, and more trees. No gators at least, but the Glades were teeming with them. Tolland didn't expect his luck to hold on that front much longer.

An ant crawled down his thumb and onto his wrist. He flicked it away, inadvertently letting go of the tree. Rocking gently on the still water, the boats drifted away until the towrope pulled taut.

The problem was he had no idea where they'd taken him. How far was he from the gulf? Had they brought him deep into the Glades or had Liddell been using the term generally, and actually stranded him somewhere within the Ten Thousand Islands? They'd driven him out from Naples with a bag over his head and the boats on a trailer hitch, but the rowboat they'd used to tow him out here had been waiting. Was there any private land out here or was it all parkland?

Never in his life had he felt so short on options. He could scream his throat raw hoping for someone to find him. He could keep working away at the ropes. He could try not to pass out from heat exhaustion or die of thirst.

If only he could scratch his goddamn itchy ass.

Tolland spat a mouthful of sticky-sweet saliva. A water strider kicked away from the frothy white glob, making tiny ripples on the surface.

Frogs chirped. High above a bald eagle shrieked. He heard a splash somewhere beyond the hammock and guessed the bird had found itself a meal.

Tolland had grown up dirt poor in a small town outside of Naples. When his father lost his job at the quarry, his mother had left them both behind. *Onward and upward*, as she'd often said. It had been a long time since he'd looked that far back but some good memories remained. Many of them involved heading out to the nearby swamp with his friends to catch frogs. Sometimes they'd use them to fish and sometimes they'd chuck them at a group of alligators—which his mother had told him was called a "congregation," as if they'd come to the swamp to worship—and they boys would marvel at the sudden feeding frenzy.

One time, he couldn't have been much older than ten, he'd been so thirsty he drank a bellyful of swamp water and ended up sick for days. His mother had told him he was lucky he didn't die. She'd said there were "microbes and such" in the water that could kill him.

Tolland knew the dangers of the Glades well.

Because of the mixture of salt water from Gulf of Mexico and fresh water from Florida Bay the Glades was home to both alligators and crocodiles. There were black bears. Poisonous snakes. Venomous spiders. Florida panthers. Wild boars. Fire ants. Vultures. At least most of these creatures couldn't swim, but there were still barracuda and gar to worry about, and even the cane toads were toxic.

And now he was trapped, alone and exposed to the elements, to all manner of hungry animal and insect, covered in honey and slowly dying of thirst.

"Fuck it," he groaned, and rocked the boat until his chin splashed into the water. He took a good mouthful, swished it around and spat it back out. The mix of salty and sweet reminded him of saltwater taffy he'd gotten from a shop on the boardwalk in Tampa when his dad had driven him out there to look for his mother. Turned out she hadn't been there, but he remembered that taffy and the trip back because his dad had gotten drunk as a skunk and Tolland had driven them back home without a license.

Tolland rocked the boat and took a huge gulp. He'd regret it later—if he lived that long. It was somewhat stagnant water but it seemed to cool off his body a few degrees inside the baking sauna of the boats.

His thirst slaked, at least temporarily, and his throat soothed, Tolland decided to put his voice to work rather than lie there like an invalid.

"HELLLLLLLLLLP!"

A flock of birds sprung from the top of the cypress, twittering excitedly as they fluttered away.

Cocking his head he listened for the concerned reply of a park ranger, an angler, a nature enthusiast—*anybody* with even a single functional ear and a pair of hands.

He waited.

His head swam from the heat. His eyes felt heavy.

Come on, you motherfucker...

Exhaustion strained every ligament, every muscle. Aristotle had kicked in the sliding glass door of Tolland's houseboat several hours before his alarm would have woken him. The man had punched him in the side of the head and kicked him in the ribs before dragging him along the dock by his hair to Liddell's idling Humvee. Then more than half an hour spent with a bag over his head in the backseat, breathing his own sweat and exhaled carbon monoxide. Then another hour or more pressed like a human Panini between the boats to get to this spot, and however long he'd already been lying here.

Tolland was exhausted but he knew he couldn't sleep.

Not like this.

Pain flared on his right foot like someone sticking a red-hot acupuncture needle into his heel and he jerked his leg, scraping the gunwale. It was far more painful than the mosquito bite. He supposed it might have been a horsefly but had nothing to gauge it against as he'd never been stung on the bottom of his foot before. Another sting came rapidly after the first and he realized he'd been holding onto a tree with this toes.

Oh fuck, not fire ants.

Tolland pushed off from the tree and used his weight to

rock the boat. Water splashed his hands and feet but several ants had already crawled into the boats and bit his ankle, his Achilles' tendon, his lower leg. Scorching pain radiated from each bite and sting.

The honey had attracted them, but how many had crawled onto his foot before that first bite? Three? Four? A dozen? *Hundreds?* As they blazed an angry red trail up his leg he remembered Aristotle's finger attacking his asshole, and the honeyed palm cupping his balls.

Oh God. Maybe they'll be fill up on dessert and leave before they get to the buffet.

His entire lower leg was on fire but the ants kept gnashing their mandibles, stabbing him with their stingers, emptying their venom sacs into every inch of exposed flesh.

Tolland's violent cursing and writhing rocked the boats. Dirty, salty water splashed into his eyes and he blinked it away. His bladder unleashed a sudden hot torrent into the bottom of the boat. He hadn't even known he'd needed to piss.

The boats, the goddamn boats—I'll never get out of here, I'LL NEVER GET OUT!

He may have made a cuckold out of Liddell, but Liddell had fucked him in the end. And Charlotte would barely register his absence.

Without realizing it, he'd begun to weep.

Somewhere in the distance an egret squawked.

Despite his pain the steady drone of flies, the swish of the trees and the gentle rocking of the boats eventually lulled Xavier Tolland to sleep.

TOLLAND WOKE with a rumbling pressure swelling his intestines, aware he'd have to shit soon. Pissing had been easy lying on his front with his penis dangling. Shitting would be a very different animal, and judging by the pain churning through his bowels it was going to be nasty.

He hadn't slept long. A few hours at most, judging by the position of the sun directly above him. Inside the boats it was so hot Tolland thought they might spontaneously combust. The morbid pessimist in him wished they would.

Beneath the ropes his skin felt like raw, bloody meat. Where the ants had attacked him was one giant continuous itch but he could ignore it if he focused. He'd spent most of his life with an itch of a sort and had only ever noticed it once Charlotte had come around to scratch it.

"*Charlotte*," Tolland moaned. He repeated it twice more as if invoking her name would make her appear. The thought that he'd never see her again, never fuck her again, was the worst thing imaginable.

Or it would have been before he'd ended up inside the boats.

A splash perked up his ears. The tendons in his neck creaked painfully as he craned to look, his bleary eyes scouring the knotted roots and low foliage surrounding his tree.

Then he saw it.

A snake—and not just any snake. Not your garden-variety garter or a water snake or even a rattler. No, this was the biggest goddamn python Tolland had ever laid eyes on outside of a zoo, its mottled green and brown body at least eight inches at its widest and as long as fifteen feet, twisting through the roots of the mangrove, only its head above the water.

"Jesus fuck!"

The snake tasted the air. Tolland had enough experience with rattlers on job sites to know the monster was searching for predators. But it also was also hunting for food.

Out here without a weapon, unable to defend himself, Tolland was the food.

His guts twisted in knots he eyed the colossal snake, willing it to move on and leave him be.

Come on, you big bastard... come onnnnnn...

The beast turned its flat head in his direction and Tolland felt his hopes dash like a man who'd lost everything on a hard eight. The python uncoiled itself from the roots and charged into the deeper water, tongue flicking, flicking.

Tolland recalled what Liddell had said about luck. If the python chomped down on his face or wrapped itself around his head and smothered him to death would it be a mercy? Could just lying here in the boats under the hot sun really be a fate worse than such a swift and brutal death?

The snake's massive length wriggled toward him like a leech, its hideous black eyes homing in on the boats.

As he waited for death Tolland noticed the insect drone had changed timbre as if in response to the presence of the slithering beast, though the flies themselves hadn't left the orbit of his head. Shifting his weight from side to side, he wobbled the boats, trying to steer them away from the giant predator—or at the very least get his head out of its reach. The water fought against him and he only managed to propel the boats backward until the towrope went taut, drawing out the agony by a few more seconds.

Literally at the end of his rope his mind suddenly seized on the buzzing.

It wasn't the flies. It was a *boat*.

Tolland began to scream, high and shrill and as loud as he could muster with his lungs compressed between the boats. He knew the vibrations would further attract the snake but he didn't care. He was dead already if he couldn't get the driver's attention. All he cared about now was getting out of the boats.

The engine roared and Tolland kept screaming as the airboat cut through the tall grass within his limited field of vision, just beyond the hammock of trees. From the corner of his eye Tolland saw the python dart away, heading back toward the mangrove. He didn't allow this small relief to quiet his cries. The tour boat was so close he could make out the individual faces of its ponchoed passengers and the white logo on the navy blue polo shirt of the driver riding high in the back.

Liddell must have left him near a tour route, the stupid rich fuck.

The airboat blew past, its propeller too loud to hear his screams, the day too bright to see into the comparatively dark cypress swamp. Even if someone had they would have seen nothing more than a pair of boats stacked one on top of each other and perhaps wondered why.

Still Tolland screamed himself hoarse at the retreating vessel.

Someone would hear him.

They would circle back. Break the padlocks. Get him out of these godforsaken boats.

Branches swished in the airboat's wake. Waves crashed against the far side of the hammock. The mangroves grumbled and swayed, unsettling birds from their branches. The sudden current upset lily pads and bent reeds on their way to the boats. The cloud of flies rose in a panicked swirl as he crashed into the big cypress, and resettled around his head when the rocking diminished.

Least it got rid of that fucking snake, he thought, swallowing a sickly-sweet mouthful of disappointment.

He knew the python would be back. It had already smelled lunch. Eventually it would come back for a taste.

Smell.

Would a snake care what its meal smelled like? If he shat himself inside the boats would the stench deter potential predators or attract them?

The pain in his guts was almost unbearable. As badly as he wanted to hold in the impending bowel movement—out of shame maybe, but mostly because he knew letting himself shit would make an already unpleasant experience even worse—Tolland had to give the idea serious consideration.

There had to be a reason, on an evolutionary level, for fear to instill a person with the urge to shit themselves.

One thing was certain, he wouldn't be able to concentrate on getting himself out of the boats with his stomach feeling like it did.

Bearing down, Tolland's innards rumbled. Maybe if he'd been lying on his back it would have been easier, or if he'd been able to raise a leg. He'd never tried to shit horizontally before. Obviously it wasn't conducive.

Before he knew it a geyser erupted from between his buttocks. It splattered against the floor of the upper boat and rained back down on him, hot and foul. Another explosive torrent oozed down between his legs, coating his dangling balls with filth. The stench wafted through the hole around his neck, prickling his nostrils. Eventually he would get used to the smell but smothered inside with the heat it would only get worse.

Only the most masochistic beast in the animal kingdom would attempt to eat him now.

He just hoped snakes could differentiate foul smells from delicious.

Already the skin between his buttocks and thighs itched. He vaguely wondered if he'd just made the biggest mistake of his life, leaving aside fucking his boss's wife. But the relief was almost glorious and he didn't intend to stick around for his excrement to attract flies and turn him into a floating maggot factory, and he certainly wouldn't hold onto the vain hope that another tour boat might pass by.

Tolland began to jerk at the ropes.

He heard a splash from the mangrove hammock and kept moving, desperate to loose his wrists. The boats were old. The wood was soft. If he could get one hand free, *just one hand*, Tolland was sure he could use the leverage to force this floating coffin apart.

The boats careened and battered against the cypress. The mooring ring jingled like a supper bell. In his periphery he saw the giant snake dart toward him. He hoped the violent movement of the boat would frighten it. And if it didn't he hoped his stink would make it think twice about eating him.

The snake inched closer, seemingly wary. Wake from the boats splashed over its head but the animal didn't retreat, it kept coming until its snout struck the side of the boat with a heavy thud between Tolland's head and his left hand.

Tolland was not a fearful man. He'd never experienced the sensation of having his heart in his throat until now. His entire body seized with terror. Adrenaline surged through his veins. The violent thrashing slowed to a gentle rock.

The snake reared back and flicked out its tongue, darted forward again and prodded the hull.

Tolland watched his fingers curl into an involuntary fist as the snake got closer and he jerked hand inward, not caring if he tore off every bit of skin and broke every bone, just wanting to get it out of reach.

The python hissed and struck.

Tolland howled in agony. Stars flooded his vision, his already limited view of the world fading to gray. Struggling to stay conscious he watched the giant reptile's tail curl under the boats.

He splayed his fingers. The reptile's head twisted back and forth as he dug his nails into the wet meat of its maw. He didn't expect the beast to choke. He merely wanted to cause it pain.

The python's tail flopped down over the side, wriggling in his face. Its massive body had curled around the boats. The devious fucker planned to break them open like a giant nut to get at the tasty morsel inside.

With an ear-splitting crunch the seats clamped down hard on his ribs, crushing the breath out of him. The hulls would split soon and he'd be free. But he'd have to fight a hungry two-hundred-pound Burmese python barehanded to get out of this goddamn swamp, and one of those hands was trapped inside the beast's mouth.

The floor of the boat split open. Stagnant water gushed in from below, splashing his chest and groin. Splintered wood gouged his thighs and exposed genitals.

Scouring the animal's mouth he found an opening and wormed his thumb inside.

Tail thrashing, slapping him in the face and beating against the hull, the snake widened and contracted its mouth around his hand but wouldn't let go. He'd plugged its airway. Hot breath whistled out around his thumb. The tail slapped down over his cheek and lay still just long enough for Tolland to gnash out and catch it in his mouth.

Bet I can swallow you before you swallow me, fucker.

With a massive crack the top of the boats caved in. Split planks tore into his back as the snake's cold, heavy body slumped over him. He felt his ankles slipped free. The tail snapped off between his teeth and he spat the raw hunk of salty meat into the swamp. The stump squirmed. Gore dripped into the water and smeared on the broken hull.

The boat sank rapidly at a sharp angle. In water up to his waist he jerked his legs against their bindings. The snake squeezed loose, splintered boards into his ribs and the gunwale tightened around his throat.

Drowned, strangled and eaten alive... They should make a Discovery Channel special about my death.

The hulls came apart and Tolland plunged into the swamp, gasping for breath. He kicked his legs free. Like a reversed crucifix the wooden seat was still lashed to his arms across his chest. Despite the fact that he'd plugged its airway the snake still tried to swallow his hand.

The python wriggled weakly around his legs, navigating jagged boards to wrap itself around him. Tolland wouldn't give it a chance. He stood on shaky limbs and waded toward his tree. Swinging himself at it with his arms outstretched, feeling like a human sprinkler, he bashed the snake's head against the cypress until its body stopped writhing and the pressure on his wrist lessened.

When the meaty pulp of the snake's head slipped off his fist and splashed lifelessly into the water, Tolland stood against the tree and tried to bring his arms together, like working the chest butterfly machine at the gym. He screamed from the exertion but the seat finally snapped in two and he stumbled forward, smashing his face into the tree.

The feeling of freedom eclipsed any pain.

He was going home.

And he wouldn't be going emptyhanded.

Tolland stood over Liddell in the dark while the man snored.

After her initial fright Charlotte had let Tolland in through the sliding glass door in the back. He'd slipped in quickly despite the extra weight on his shoulders. The walk along the tour route through the hammocks had been strenuous but once he'd reached a main road it wasn't long before an amused man in a pickup pulled over to marvel at him. When Tolland had told him what he'd planned the man had eagerly let him jump in the back and had driven him all the way back to Naples.

"Just keep that damn thing away from me," he'd said, and Tolland had.

Now he stood over Liddell while the swimming pool threw ripples of light over the art on the walls and the man himself snored, sleeping the sleep of a man at peace with the world.

"Hello, Liddell."

The man roused slowly. Finally he raised his head toward the intruder and drew up hurriedly on his elbows.

"Tolland? Is that you?"

Tolland couldn't see the man's expression in the dim light but the edge of fear was a treat. "Don't bother calling Aristotle. Charlotte woke him with that little dueling pistol of yours."

"What do you want? What is that awful *smell?*"

"You know, I thought about all the things I would do to you on the way back from the Glades. What do you get for the man who has everything?" Tolland asked in a jovial tone. "Then I remembered how much you like animals."

He let the python unfurl with a heavy thud onto Liddell's four-poster bed.

The man crawled back against the headboard with a squeak of fear, clutching the covers to his scrawny chest. "*What is that?*"

Grinning, Tolland slipped the kitchen knife Charlotte had handed him out from his belt and dragged it up the body of the snake. The reptile's stinking guts spilled out in cold wet clumps over Liddell's satin bedsheets. Immediately the man began to retch.

"Did you know a Burmese python will wrap itself around a boat and crack it like a nut?"

Tolland let the python drop into the bed. Its battered head flopped down between the white satin tents made by Liddell's legs.

"Jesus!" Liddell cried, kicking the thing away, but it was too heavy to budge. He retched again, bringing a hand up to cover his mouth. Puke spewed through his fingers, pattering on the bedsheets and a hundred pounds of snake guts.

Tolland laughed. "I guess I'm pretty lucky after all, huh, Liddell? And now you know how Charlotte felt sharing her bed with a snake like you."

He left the man vomiting.

NOTES: "The Boats" was my entry into the *VS:X* anthology, in which a writer from the U.S. (or Canada, in my case) went head to head with a writer from the U.K. in an "extreme" horror short story contest. I was paired against Michael Bray, whose admittedly brilliant story was a fake autobiographical account of his jealousy toward me and my subsequent murder. It was voted on first by judges then by readers. Mine lost in both regards I believe, though since Bray's story was my first time being murdered in a work of fiction, part of me feels like I still won.

The anthology also marked a high point for me as I believe it might have been what put me on legendary horror author Jack Ketchum's radar. He ended up reading my debut collection *Gristle & Bone* and having some kind words to say about it, which was mind-blowing, to say the least.

PRICK

There was no escaping it: Zoey's date was a giant dick. Within the span of an hour, he'd insulted their server, poked fun at Zoey's outfit, and shushed her to catch a baseball replay. Before the drinks arrived, he'd already oh-so-casually touched her shoulder three times in an obvious attempt to create intimacy, had set his phone down between them and regularly checked incoming text messages, and had talked over her twice to one-up her admittedly well-worn but still humorous anecdotes. Worse, he'd interrupted the answer to a question he himself had asked—as if he'd been checking it off a list—to tell her about his previous long-term girlfriend who was, according to him, a "certified crazy bitch."

Zoey Esprit knew his ploy. She'd experienced it in some form or another a dozen times, at least. Modern dating was a labyrinthine manscape riddled with trolls, bros, haters, and selfie-obsessed *divos*. It took a thick skin to find a good man swimming in an ocean of losers. Sometimes she felt like she'd been trying to find a specific needle in a *stack* of needles, where every attempt drew a potential prick.

Still, she had to put herself "out there." A girl could only Netflix and Chill by herself so much before friends and family started to think she must be frigid.

She'd met a few decent guys using dating apps, but more and more it seemed like dick pics had become a standard greeting. In the past month alone, she'd seen enough crooked, small, overly hairy, warted and/or ugly penises to make the publishers of *Playgirl* blush.

And then came Orson.

Zoey had been drunk, depressed, and maybe a little horny when they'd met on the elevator, after a night she'd spent dancing with the girls, and Orson had oh-so-casually slipped into her messy life like a Trojan horse with a slightly witty comment she no longer remembered. He'd been clever and intelligent and thoughtful during their brief conversations in the lobby and elevators since, and her defenses had fallen like the army of Troy.

She realized her error now, sitting at this sports bar across from this handsome yet socially repugnant man with Buffalo wing sauce smeared on his lips and chin, who bumped his cheap draft beer with an elbow, nearly spilling it as he made to cheer a homerun from whichever team was "his." She'd mistaken the fact that he'd been different from the pervs and assholes she'd encountered in her most recent experiences on social media with him being in a much higher echelon, when in reality he was likely far lower. At least those other men, sleazy as they were, were honest about it.

Attempting to slip out as casually as possible without causing a scene, Zoey grabbed her purse. It took a moment for Orson to snap his focus away from the game on the big screen behind her and notice she was slipping out of the booth.

"Where are you going?"

"Bathroom," she said, and flashed him an awkward smile.

Orson wiped his fingers on the stack of napkins. "You're taking your purse?"

Caught, Zoey shrugged and said the only thing she could think to diffuse the situation: "Tampons."

He glanced down at the splotches of red sauce on the napkins beside his plate. "That's cool," he said with a shrug. "I'm an enlightened guy. I also don't mind taking a ride down the Red River, if you know what I mean."

Zoey didn't bother concealing her disgust. "Good to know," she said, and wound through tables of sports fans toward the bathrooms.

The doors were in the other direction, but she'd already decided to head out the back, and while customers high-fived each other, raucously cheering another homerun—or something—no one heard the commotion in the kitchen as she hurried through on her way to the exit.

"No, DON'T STROKE IT," she told him. "I wanna feel it get hard in my mouth."

Orson cursed himself for calling Gina, but after he'd been ditched at the Wing Zone, none of his regular booty call fallbacks had answered any of his texts. Gina had messaged back immediately, almost as though she'd been *waiting* for him to text—despite the fact that he'd broken it off with her weeks ago.

Probably was, the crazy bitch.

Orson stopped tugging to let her slurp it into her mouth like a hot noodle. It thickened as she sucked, growing fat on her tongue, filling her mouth, and he began to forget about that bitch from the eighth floor sticking him with the bill for her appetizers and drinks. Losing himself to pre-orgasmic bliss.

He was only semi-erect when Gina's teeth grazed his flesh. Not hard, just playfully. Still, he yelped.

"Hey, watch the teeth!"

Her lips curled up in a smile around his fattened schlong, ice blue, heavy-lidded eyes wild with malevolent glee. She tossed her curly hair over her shoulder and took his cock in her hand to suck on his balls, a little harder than he liked.

Orson moaned—whether despite or because of the pain, he wasn't sure. His smooth ball popped from of her lips.

"Why do you sleep with all those whores?" she asked him, beginning to squeeze his wet cock between her tits.

"What whores? What are you talking about?"

"I've been watching you, Orson. All those women... do you *love* them? Do you love them like you loved me?" She let a runnel of spit dribble down onto the head of his prick.

Orson might have corrected her, might have told her he'd never loved her, had she not started stroking him between her perfect tits. Hard to concentrate. Difficult to focus on anything but the rhythm and the heat.

"*Ffffuck yeah!*" he moaned.

And she bit.

Hard.

Orson screamed, pushing against the top of her head, but Gina's teeth held him firm, like a dog on a bone. Something hot and wet splashed against his abdomen, and for a moment he thought it was spit or even vomit, but the pain was so enormous, so *all-encompassing* that he knew it must be blood, and he kicked at her, striking her flat stomach and smooth thighs with his knees, but her bite held, and he punched her temples and pounded on the top of her head, and still her teeth met in the middle with a pronounced *clack*, the blood vessels and urethra snapping, and she rose from his groin—he was blacking out now, thank fuck—smiling gleefully, her cheeks puffed out like a chipmunk's, the lower half of her face covered in his blood, before she strode stark naked to the open window and spat his cock out into the cool night air.

By the time she'd slammed the window, Orson was unconscious.

——————

THE OLD MAN whom residents of Alton Towers called the T.P. Man, because his rickety shopping cart was always loaded with toilet paper, heard the screaming from above moments before something splashed into the puddle at his feet.

The T.P. Man grunted sleepily on the bench and looked down, peering into the shallow, gritty black water. Looked like a bird had fallen out of the sky, wings folded around its body. Or a fat, giant slug. Nothing of particular interest, until it *squirmed*.

He pulled his feet from the puddle, drawing his knees to his chest. The movement had startled him. Blinking his bleary eyes until it came into focus, he gave the object a closer look.

Some lady threw her vibrator out the window, the T.P. Man thought, watching the floppy pink thing splash.

"Bit small for a dildo," he remarked. "Must be for the backdoor. Or a junior Miss."

The T.P. Man chuckled, and began to push his shopping cart full of Charmin toward the above ground parking garage. In about an hour, security would be around to harass him, but he knew of a spot behind the garage where teenagers hung out to smoke their wacky weed during the day. A kind of clubhouse, where he could sleep until dawn.

Behind him, the splashes stopped.

He turned, expecting to see the vibrator in the still water, having run out its batteries. But the puddle was empty. The vibrator had disappeared.

"Some raccoon run away with it," he said. "Havin' himself a raccoon sex party."

He laughed again, pushing the cart down the round-about. Damn back wheel was spinning again. Need to get that fixed or it'd get hard to push to the grocery store and back for his weekly stock of Charmin.

A tin can clattered in the gutter at his feet. The T.P. Man startled, looking down in time to see a small shape scurry into the bushes. Probably a rat. His nose wrinkled from the sour smell of urine. Drunk residents pissed in the bushes here sometimes on their way home from wherever, because they knew the Super would just blame it on old Rufus, the T.P. Man.

"Got more respect for myself than that," Rufus said haughtily. "Prob'ly pin all that dog shit on me too, if they could."

Rufus used the woods nearby when he needed to go. He'd built a small outhouse toilet out of scrap wood, and dug the pit himself.

"Good enough for the Pope, it's good enough for me," he said, and chuckled.

Low branches shook, leaves swishing as the rodent scurried on ahead of him.

Go on, little rat, Rufus thought as he wheeled the cart around the side of the garage, onto the dirt-floored "clubhouse." *You handle your business, I'll handle mine.*

"Speaking of 'business,'" the T.P. Man said, and grabbed a roll of toilet paper from the stack. Felt like it'd be a firm one today, which was good. The older he got, the runnier *they* got. Of course, his diet—or lack of it—didn't help firm things up much.

Rufus left his cart and trekked out into to the woods. He picked up a cigarette butt from the ditch on the way. The parkland was dark, at probably around one or two in the A.M., but not so dark he couldn't see. City dark never got much darker than a hospital ward, but the canopy of trees blocked out much of the moonlight, and his poor vision made it worse.

Unseen animals scurried in the underbrush. An occasional vehicle swished by along the highway. Otherwise, the night was still and quiet.

Rufus found his toilet. He untied his belt, pulled down his grimy, loose jeans and tattered undies, and squatted over the two weather-dampened planks that served as a seat, resting the toilet paper beside him. He straightened the stubbed cigarette, smeared with red lipstick, and lit it with a scratched pink Bic lighter.

Hard work tonight, more like birthing a baby. Just when he thought he'd never make and he'd have to go to sleep with an uncomfortable pain in his guts, his bowels loosened, and two fat turds fell into the pit with a crunch of dry leaves.

The T.P. Man tore off four squares of paper, folded them in two, and wiped. When he'd had a home, he'd liked to give himself what he'd called a "spray-lo," using the deodorizer to spray a halo around himself and his stink, but out here in the semi-wild the smell wafted itself away. He bunched up the used paper and tossed it into the hole.

He'd pulled his pants to his knees when the poop suddenly and violently squeezed through his anus, tearing at the delicate skin. Rufus cried out in surprise. He didn't like to be surprised, least of all by a sneak attack turd.

Only this turd seemed to be going *in*, and not *out*.

The T.P. Man leaped to his feet, feeling the shameful sting of sexual violation as whatever it was worked its way into his asshole. He'd been raped before, by two boys from the college who'd called him degrading names while they did it. It had taken plenty of rubbing alcohol to get beyond that trauma. Cost him most of his sight and probably half of his liver.

Rufus jerked around, looking for his attacker—but the woods around him were dark, and seemingly empty. Still, the fat thing wormed upward, like a shit that forgot the way. He felt it squirming inside him, while the pain in his anus lessened, though he felt blood—or shit—trickle down his inner thigh.

Meanwhile, he felt the thing—*L'il Miss's dildo? A rat?*—squeeze into his guts.

"Oh God, I'm gonna—"

Rufus puked, strings of bile splattering on his dusty jacket sleeve. He staggered forward, tripping on the pants around his ankles, sent sprawling headlong in the dirt. The thing was in his esophagus now—felt like a mouthful of food gone down the wrong way.

He swallowed hard, hoping to dislodge it, but it only

worked its way further along, horizontal now, wriggling toward his throat.

Be over soon, at least. Damn thing prob'ly just wants out, and I ain't about stop it!

It stopped moving. Rufus made to gasp in relief, but it had plugged his airway. Couldn't breathe. Couldn't scream, the thing pressed against his vocal cords.

Tears streaming down his face, Rufus reached into his mouth, dirty fingernails scrabbling over his tongue, pushing past his uvula, scouring the back of his throat for the animal, whatever it was.

Without a voice to scream, the T.P. Man merely squirmed and moaned, rustling in the dead leaves at the foot of his makeshift toilet until he was dead.

On a torrent of shit and vomit, something small and plump oozed out of the T.P. Man's mouth, plopping softly onto a scattered pile of leaves.

A moment later, it was slithering through the woods toward the tall black pillar of sparkling golden lights where it was born.

———

ZOEY HAD MET Dan at a business event, and though she'd found him a tad posh, they had hit it off almost immediately.

It had been a month since her awful date with Orson Ladd, on a night the residents of Alton Towers now referred to as "The Night It Happened." Few would say aloud what "it" meant, but they all knew: a crazy woman had bitten off Orson's penis and spat it out the window of his fifteenth story apartment. The woman had fled, but police had caught her at her apartment, enjoying a glass of chilled Chablis. EMTs had earlier carted Orson off to the hospital, unconscious from shock and blood loss. And after an extensive search, the appendage was never found.

It.

Zoey felt a little guilty for what had happened to Orson, though she knew she wasn't to blame. If she hadn't skipped out on him—a cowardly act, admittedly—he might not have felt compelled to bring home the "certified crazy bitch" (Zoey had remembered her first name, Gina, which had corresponded with the name in the papers), and might still at this moment be intact.

Then Zoey had met Dan, and their blossoming relationship had taken her mind off of Orson Ladd and his missing piece.

She wasn't in love with Dan, no yet. But there had been an attraction there from the start. She supposed the accent had some to do with it; she'd always been a sucker for a sexy Englishmen.

At the end of their first date, he'd kissed her. For their third date, she'd brought him back to her apartment, and after cooking him dinner, they'd slept together.

"Fucking odd, isn't it?" Dan said over coffee—he had tea—at the shop across the street when they met the following Monday. "I mean, who would rape a homeless person? Can you imagine the *stench*?"

The homeless man who sometimes loitered in the foyer had been found dead in the woods nearby. The news said he'd been raped. The thought that it had happened so close to her apartment terrified Zoey.

"Can we talk about something else, please?"

Dan pushed the Jaffa Cake he'd brought around his plate, barely touched. "It's just so... *unsavory*. Honestly, I don't think I can eat." This seemed to tickle him. "That's rather ironic, isn't it? Being unable to eat because of a homeless man? Because of the starving thing, I mean."

"Yeah, I got it."

Dan gave her a look. "Are you angry, Zo?"

"I'm not angry, I'm upset."

"I don't understand the difference."

"I'm upset about that man," she said. "Rufus."

"Rufus!" Dan said, delighted. "On a first name basis with the Tee Pee Man, were you?"

Zoey threw her napkin on the table and gave him an icy glare as he leaned back in his chair, blowing on his tea. "You know, you can be really rude sometimes."

"Look, I'm sorry, Zoey. It's just that everyone is suddenly concerned with this guy when up until last week nobody gave a shit about him. I mean, did anyone go out of their way to find out why he was sleeping behind the garage? Did anyone offer him a hot meal or a bath?"

"That's not the point."

"I'd rather say that *is* the point. If he hadn't been squatting in the woods—*literally*, according to the news—he wouldn't have been in the woods that night for some deranged lunatic to rape and murder. God, I hope they used *protection*..." He pulled a disgusted face.

"You're being callous."

"Well, I don't see you out there, giving alms to the poor."

The bell dinged above the door before she could reply, and a man shuffled in, hunched and bedraggled, dressed in a baggy gray tracksuit. He walked with a hobble up to the counter, and ordered a grandé macchiato. Zoey recognized his drink before his voice, which was cracked, the hard edge softened.

"Orson?"

He half-glanced over his shoulder, keeping himself hidden under the hood.

"Orson, it's me." She went to his side. "Zoey."

Begrudgingly, he turned. His eyes were sunken, hollowed out. Like he'd dragged himself through hell and back.

"Hi, Zoey," he said, his voice small.

"Orson!" Dan giggled. "*The* Orson?" He approached them at the counter, chuckling as he stuck out a hand. "Zoey has told me a lot about you. How are you, then? You know... down there."

Orson looked down at the crotch of Dan's pants. "How are *you* down there? Or should I ask you?" he said, turning his inquiring look on Zoey.

"I just wanted to apologize—"

"*Don't*," Orson said. "There's nothing to apologize for. In fact, the transplant's bigger than what I had before. I'm *happy* it happened."

His order came up. He took his drink, and shouldered past Dan. Dan watched him the whole way with an amused grin.

"D'you think that's true? You know, that it's bigger?"

Zoey left Dan standing at the counter.

She was still thinking about their tiff—Dan would call it a *row*—when the superintendent came into the mailroom, startling her.

"Yeah hi, Zoey, hi," he said over his bifocals. He had his tool bag with him, and like usual, he seemed busy and a little flustered. Zoey often wondered whether it was because his position was paid for by the tenants, that he was putting on a show to justify his paycheck.

"Hi, Mr. Popadopolous. Busy today?"

"I'll rest when I'm dead. Your pipes okay?"

"As far as I know. Is there a problem?"

Mr. Popadopolous leafed through his own mail. "Just some clogged toilets on the lowers floors. Real mess. You have any problems, you be sure and let me know," he said, and tossed the entire stack of mail in the recycle bin.

"I will, thank you."

As they waited for the elevators—the service one was out again, though she didn't mention this to Mr. Popadopolous—he turned to her briefly. "You don't happen to know anyone who owns a snake in the building, do you?"

"A snake?"

"You know..." The portly bald man flicked out his tongue and made a hissing sound between his teeth.

"I can think of a few men who'd fit that description, Mr. Popadopolous, but no, not the animal. Why do you ask?"

He shrugged. "Eh, no reason."

Elevator two opened. Mr. Popadopolous limped in. "Take care of yourself, Zoey."

"You too, Mr. Popadopolous."

As the doors closed behind him, elevator one opened, and she stepped inside.

———

Stavros Popadopolous, known as "Pop" to family and friends, stepped out of the elevator into the cool basement. "Snaaaake..." he called. "Oh, snaaaake!"

There was no reply. Not that a snake could reply even if it wanted to.

Two residents had claimed to have glimpsed a snake in

the basement, and another had seen... *something*... in the parking garage. Pop hadn't let it bother him until he'd seen the LOST CAT poster on the message board in the lobby, and found the cat itself in the boiler room a few hours later, having lost a lot of blood from small bites all over its body.

Either it had been ganged up on by a pack of hungry rats, or there really was a snake loose in the building. Pop had seen *Snakes on a Plane* and had no interest in playing Samuel L. Jackson.

"Sna-*aaaaaake*?"

Mrs. Bartleby stepped out of the laundry room lugging an empty plastic hamper, and Pop nearly shit a brick.

"Oh! Jeez! You scared me, Mrs. Bartleby."

"You scare too easy, Stavros," the elderly woman said, and she gave him a good-natured slap on the shoulder. "Man up!"

"Ha ha, yeah, I guess I probably should. Have a good day, Mrs. Bartleby."

Truthfully, Pop was still shaken from what had happened in apartment 1303, the night he'd seen the door wide open and found Orson Ladd passed out naked on his bed in a puddle of blood, his "little Ladd" bitten off and spat out the window by some crazy woman.

Pop relaxed a little as he continued into the laundry room, and gaped at what he saw. The floor was covered in water. The drain in the center of the tiled floor gurgled.

"Dammit," he muttered, and searched for the source of the spill, cursing Mrs. Bartleby under his breath. Her laundry rattled in one of the dryers, the only one running this morning.

The spill had originated under the oldest of the frontload washing machines. Pop grabbed a dirty towel from the wash basin and laid it down, then knelt on it. The bottom of the tub was full of dingy water when he opened the door. He removed the drain panel with his socket wrench, and a small clump of gummy, wet pinkish gray lint oozed out from the hole. It made Pop think of afterbirth. Too small to have caused the mess though, whatever it looked like.

He scooped away the wet lint, and leaned his head into the tub, hoping to get a better look at the clog. Cavernous drips arose from the drainpipe, which lead straight back for a good three feet into the utility room, where it shot down into the ground, and to the sewers below, he assumed. He took out his flashlight and shined it into the dark hole.

Dingalingalingaling!

His cell phone rang in its hip holster, and Pop startled, banging his head on the inside of the washer with a giant *gongggg!*

He pulled his head out and rubbed his shiny scalp, thinking Mrs. Bartleby may have been right about "manning up."

One more scare like that and the old ticker's gonna give up the ghost, he thought, wondering if he'd remembered to take his blood thinners this morning. He was always forgetting since Muriel passed two years ago last spring.

Pop picked up the phone. It was the exterminator he'd called. The man was booked solid for the next two days, but he promised to come the following morning. Sounded like a stand-up guy, and he'd been recommended.

He put his phone on silent, holstered it, and reached into the drainpipe. Fingers roaming the width of the pipe, feeling damp, cool metal, and small clumps of lint, they finally came to rest on something warm and spongy.

Blood pumped under its flesh. It was *alive.*

The snake bit his finger before he could retract his hand,

the pain more terrible than anything he'd felt before, even when he'd caught a chunk of shrapnel in the calf from a cluster bomb in Vietnam—which had been every bit as excruciating as it sounds.

Pop pulled back from the tub with a scream, blood dripping onto his lap. The end of his index finger had been bit clean off at the second knuckle, revealing pink muscle and white bone. He fell back on his ass in the puddle, holding his injured finger, staring into the small black hole at the back of the washing machine as he wrapped his hand with the damp towel.

The snake in the pipe launched at him. Pop's mouth opened wide in terror, and it lodged in his throat, silencing his scream. He grasped the fleshy thing with his uninjured hand, pull at the snake as it wriggled and squirmed, trying to slither down his throat and lay eggs in his stomach, like his grandmother had often warned him they would when he was a boy.

Pop jerked it from his mouth and gasped for breath, holding it away from his face as it thrashed in his hand.

His eyes went wide.

It wasn't a snake—it was a *penis*. A *human* penis, about ten inches in length and at least two wide, flopping in his hand like a dildo left too close to the radiator. He threw it at the wall—more out of disgust than fear—and tried to get to his feet.

His boots slipped in the puddle, and he fell on his back, cracking a rib, loosing his breath in a pained gasp. Pop lay there, stunned and terrified, unable to move without further damaging his rib, praying for someone, *anyone*, to come downstairs and help him up.

The buzzing dryer alarm snapped him back to reality.

There was no penis, only a slightly large, very violent snake. He'd stunned it when it struck the wall, and hopefully it wouldn't risk another attack. But he couldn't count on it. Mrs. Bartleby's clothes tumbled as the drum rolled to a stop, and Pop tried to ease himself up.

The creature slapped wetly against his cheek. Pop reared back his head as far as he could, the pain in his ribs excruciating. He saw the thing—a penis, no doubting the wet slit in its mottled purple head, or the thick roll of foreskin—inch toward him out of the corner of his eye.

With the last of his strength, he cried out for "HELLLLLLP!"

The sentient penis plunged into the dark, hairy cove of his ear, and before Stavros Popadopolous could even *think* about shitting bricks, the monster penetrated his brain with a very loud *POP!*

LANA MATHER SAT in an uncomfortable chair the Sexual Health Clinic, nursing her sore stomach.

It had been hurting since yesterday morning, when she'd taken the walk of shame back home from the apartment of that guy she'd met on Tinder. She'd downed a few drinks to "get over herself" (heeding her girlfriend Trina's advice), and had taken an Uber to his building. She couldn't even remember his first name, let alone the last.

He was good-looking, at least, though with the lights dimmed she supposed he might not have been a stunner in the daylight. Not that his looks had mattered much. What had mattered was that he'd been slightly less disgusting than most of the men she and Trina had surveyed on her app, while downing tequila shots.

She'd never done anything like it before, but after Hunter had cheated on her, she'd felt like she needed to get a few bangs with randos out of her system, and Trina had agreed. Especially since Lana still planned on marrying Hunter in the spring.

"Miss Mather?"

Lana looked up from the magazine she'd been pretending to read. Other than her, two older women sat looking at their phones, trying to avoid looking at the pervy guy in the far corner, who wore sunglasses.

"The doctor will see you now," the secretary said. "Have a seat in room three, she'll be with you in a moment."

Lana stood, and made her way to the open examination room near the back of the building. She sat in the chair, and studied STD warning posters while she awaited the doctor.

Lana was surprised it was her stomach that hurt now and not her throat, battered and bruised by the guy's huge cock— way too big to take "balls deep" (another gem from Trina) into her petite pussy. Or her cervix, which he'd treated like a fat lady with a display shoe during a buy-one-get-one sale, causing her to shift uncomfortably on the subway and behind her desk at work all throughout the following day. She'd thought at first that was why she felt sick, since she'd swallowed his cum—a decision she'd immediately regretted, though she had only done it so he wouldn't cum in her hair, leaving traces for Hunter to find. But when she'd thrown up later that night, she'd known her problems were far worse.

She and Hunter had been snuggled under the covers watching Jimmy Fallon last night when a sudden wave of queasiness had overcome her. She'd flipped back the blanket and scurried to the en suite, where she'd thrown up as quietly as she did after a large meal, so Hunter wouldn't hear.

"Y'okay, beb?" Hunter had called.

Lana had cleared her throat, blinking tears away to look into the bowl. What she'd seen amid chunks of semi-digested sandwich made her throw up again.

Before she could explore the terrifying thoughts swimming through her mind, Lana had flushed the toilet, hoping she'd puked up the last of it. Still, she'd tossed and turned all night, barely getting a wink of sleep, and she'd gone to the clinic first thing in the morning, after Hunter had left for work.

The doctor entered, a small brown-haired woman in jeans, with a nametag on the breast of her t-shirt. She sat in the chair opposite, and gave poor miserable Lana a sympathetic look. "Hi... Lana, is it? What seems to be the problem?"

Lana swallowed hard—much like she wished she hadn't two nights ago. "I had unprotected sex," she said. "With a stranger. And now my stomach's sore."

"I see." The doctor drew her feet up onto the chair, holding the toes of her shoes in a childlike way. "Do you think you may be pregnant?"

"*Pregnant?* Oh God, no!" Lana chuckled nervously. "I mean, I *hope* not."

"Then why are you here, Lana?"

"I'm wondering... is it possible for sperm to have..." She felt lame asking, like an ignorant kid on WebMD. "... parasites?"

The doctor looked at her askance. "Parasites?"

"I swallowed," Lana said. Her mind flashed on what she'd seen in the toilet bowl last night. *Maggots.* Dozens of them. Little pink wriggly things with purple heads, worming through chewed bits of bread and cheese and lettuce and sliced ham.

Recalling the image made her nearly faint, and she stood abruptly, rushing to the sink, where she vomited again and again, hundreds of little pinkish parasites with purple heads squirming over each other in the flat bottom of the shiny metal sink.

She stood over it, catching her breath as she wiped her mouth, her throat raw.

The doctor gasped behind her, scaring her worse than the sink full of parasites.

"What's wrong with me...?" Lana cried, but the doctor was already backing away from her in horror.

MELISSA JOHNSON WAS SUFFERING through the worst cramps of her life.

She'd downed three Midol with a glass of vodka rocks, and still her ovaries kicked the shit out of her. Now the hangover was kicking in to boot, and her shoulders and head throbbed while her insides felt like a riding lawn-mower was churning up her uterus and spewing it out of her vagina.

Melissa went to the toilet, certain her current tampon was no longer viable. She unzipped her jeans, slid down the old stained period panties, and sat on the toilet.

She planted her bare feet on the cold tile on either side of the toilet, and pulled the string.

The sodden tampon slid out, splashing drops of blood into the bowl that swirled into dark red whorls as they struck.

Melissa made to reach for the toilet paper when a

painful, bloody torrent spewed from her, splashing into the cold water like a violent bout of diarrhea.

When the flood stopped, she ventured a mortified look into the bowl.

What she saw there, thrashing, splashing in the murky water, made her slip off the toilet as her vision grayed, and as she fell she tore down the shower curtain, striking her head on the porcelain tub.

ORSON SPAT into his hand and worked the goober over the bulbous head of his massive new prick.

Her asshole winked at him, a clean, tight pucker. He stuck in his moistened thumb, working it around inside as she moaned.

Orson thrust the penis into her and plowed away without much enthusiasm, his date moaning and writhing under his weight, pulling him down to the mattress. Sex would never be like it was before the Night It Happened.

Still, he'd learned over the past month to take pleasure in his partners' pleasure. He'd had to. Mentally, he was all there. "In the moment," as they say. Blood seemed to flow to it correctly and the penis stayed erect—much longer than it used to—but the feeling wasn't quite there. It was a foreign entity. Like using a strap-on dildo, or waving with a phantom arm.

The woman rolled over onto her back, rotating with it still inside of her. A move like that would have put him over the top before, but his new penis just craved more. When it finally did come, Orson only felt a ghost of what he would have felt before the injury. It was better than nothing, so he didn't complain. He just brought home more women, and let his penis have its way with them.

He no longer controlled himself. A slave to his prick, he merely did its bidding. At least before he'd been doing it for himself, or had lived under the pretense it was for himself, when really he'd been bound by his obsession.

He wished he'd never called Gina that night. And because he had, he wished Gina hadn't left the door open and Pop had never found him.

He wished he'd died instead.

She grabbed his hand and moved it toward her. Orson fishhooked two fingers into her pussy while his prick battered the inside of her colon, his thumb rubbing her clit, the pads of his fingers pressing against her g-spot until he felt the walls of her cunt contract, and as she cried out in ecstasy his monster cock spewed a huge load into her asshole like a kid puking off a rollercoaster.

He rolled off of her, the penis still rock hard.

"Oh my God, Orson," she breathed, lighting the joint she'd left on the bedside table. "Your big dick is amazing. *Ugly*—but amazing."

"The surgeon said it belonged to a serial killer," he said.

She blew smoke out of her nose in disbelief. *"What?"*

"Yeah. They said he was a real pussy slayer."

The woman laughed. He didn't even remember her name, just some professional-looking blonde woman he'd picked up at a nearby bar, who'd been so obviously craving a good fuck it was like he could smell her desire. Or his new cock could. It had started throbbing at the mere sight of her, full of Big Dick Energy, like a dowsing rod leading him toward water. Like a GPS homing in on her pussy, and finally, her ass.

He almost felt a sense of relief inside of her warm holes, that same feeling he'd been chasing ever since he'd gotten his first handjob when he was thirteen years old, from his best friend's mom behind the bleachers, while the other boys kicked a ball around like blissful idiots.

Like it was *home*.

⸻

REPORTS OF WOMEN experiencing unusually heavy periods over the past several weeks had gone mostly unnoticed by those in the medical community, and the string of deaths of menstruating women from heart attacks, car accidents, and severe internal bleeding—not to mention ulcers—were never linked by local news media.

Meanwhile, the incidents of clogged toilets around the city rose exponentially. Plumbers were glad for the extra business—all except one, who'd been splashed in the eye while snaking an elderly woman's shitter, and had waked in the night unable to see out of it. He'd gone to the bathroom to find a messy pulp of slime running down his cheek from his puckered eyelids, and stared at it in horror with his working eye.

When the small penis erupted from the eye socket, squirming out like a worm from an apple, Lorne Jameson suffered his third coronary, and his last thoughts as he writhed on the bathroom floor were to curse his wife, who'd often told him, "I swear to God, Lorne, you're gonna die in front of somebody's toilet!"

Which he did.

⸻

PRICK SLEPT in the ducts close to the boiler, where the air was warm and dry.

Life was difficult for the most part, ever since Fuck Yeah had bitten off its tail, separating it from God Orson. When Prick wasn't feeding, it spent most of its time lurking in the nooks and crannies and pipes and ductwork of the place where it was born, hiding from the bipedal giants and their furry minions.

This morning, several days after it had penetrated the old bald giant's ear and nested a while in the squishy warmth of his brain, Prick had spent hours worming through the water pipes, splashing up into urine bowls and trailing cold water onto the floors as it slithered into bedrooms, living rooms and kitchens, searching for food. Prick had been consuming a bowl half filled with soggy cereal when the sound of footsteps startled it, and Prick slithered away, spilling the bowl onto the table, and hid under the counter.

The female giant had screamed and chased Prick with a broom through an opened vent, into the next apartment.

Prick could sense God Orson's presence above, and had often communed with Him since they'd been separated. It was about the only pleasure Prick got now, aside from feeding, but its communions with God Orson, while miraculous, were also full of pain.

Prick had inched its way through the empty apartment, climbing counters and onto sofas, finding nothing of sustenance, and had finally slipped into an opened drawer full of bunched underwear, or what Prick had once called "prisons of cloth," until Prick had realized being nestled in the Groin of the Father had been a privilege, not a penance.

Prick had found a box of rubbers among the underwear, what female bipedal giants often called "protection," alongside a small plastic bottle, its cap removed, the blue candy contents spilled out on the bottom of the drawer. The candy had tasted bitter, but Prick had eaten every last one.

And now, as it molted inside the warm duct, shedding the dried-out husk of its too-small skin, Prick's belly grew fat once more.

God Orson the Creator did not know that Prick was female.

He did not know that she was *spawning*.

———

"I'M THE EXTERMINATOR. Sorry I'm late."

Acting as temporary Superintendent until someone was hired to take the place of the dearly departed, Mrs. Bartleby shook the man's hand and welcomed him to the building.

"What happened to Pop?" the small, slim man in baggy blue coveralls asked.

Mrs. Bartleby looked upwards, thumbing the crucifix around her neck. "He passed, God rest him."

"Oh. That sucks," the exterminator said.

Mrs. Bartleby leaned in close and whispered, "*The rats* got him. At least, that's what I suspect. Crawled right into his ear and chewed a hole in his brain." The exterminator gave her a disbelieving look, and she thumbed her crucifix once more. "So you see, the problem is quite urgent."

"Well, that's why I'm here. You got nothing to worry about, ma'am. I'll find your rats, and I'll kill 'em too. That's my motto," he added, showing her his toolkit, on which the motto was stenciled: I FIND YOUR PESTS AND I KILL THEM TOO!

"Wonderful," Mrs. Bartleby said, rubbing her hands

together enthusiastically. "*When* they are dead, I'd like to see the corpses, if that isn't too much of a bother. Mr. Popadopolous—Aristotle—was a dear dear friend, and I'd very much like to know the creature responsible—or *creatures*—are disposed of in a most *in*humane manner."

"Well, that's why I'm here," the exterminator repeated.

"Thank you," Mrs. Bartleby said, touching his arm.

Alvin the Exterminator looked down at her wrinkled hand on his coverall sleeve with distaste until she removed it. "No trouble at all, ma'am," he said finally.

Mrs. Bartelby thanked him, gave him the master keys, and shuffled off to the elevators.

Once the crazy old bat was on her way up, Alvin got down on his hands and knees in front of the register in the foyer, listening to the *tick tick tick* of heat pumping through the duct, his hair blowing lightly in its warmth.

He detected no scent of urine in the air flow, and thumbed the down button for the elevators. Best to check the basement first, before dealing with the old lady again.

Chewed into his brain, he thought, remembering the old broad's words. That was nothing to Alvin. He'd seen a woman chewed to death by rats. He'd seen a man's flesh come alive, wriggling from an infestation of larvae under the skin. He'd seen a basement so filled with orb weavers and cobwebs it was like walking onto the set of a horror movie. He'd even seen a mythical "rat king," a pile of eighteen rats all knotted together at the tail, squeaking and tearing at each other to get free.

Nothing here he wouldn't have seen a hundred times before.

The basement was cool and dimly lit. No smell here,

either. Alvin trusted his nose implicitly. If there were rats in the building, he'd have smelled them by now.

A teenaged girl wearing tight-fitting pink jogging pants with JUICY stenciled on the bum stood in the laundry room, tossing handfuls of frilly underwear in reds and blacks into a mesh hamper. He watched her bend to the dryer again, her buttocks jiggling pleasantly, before she popped up and caught him staring. He nodded at her, but she sneered, so Alvin moved on to the boiler room.

He smelled damp concrete, and a very faint sour smell that might have been rat piss, but it definitely wasn't fresh. As far as Alvin was concerned, there hadn't been a rat in this building for a few weeks, maybe even longer. He checked the corners, where dust and dirt and cobwebs had collected, looking for rat turds and finding nothing.

There were some dried insects, but otherwise, it was the cleanest building he'd ever encountered.

"Better check the ducts, just to be safe."

Alvin set his tool kit on the floor, opened it, and removed a multi-bit screwdriver. Too short to reach the ducts on foot, he returned to the hall where he'd seen a plastic milk crate. Standing on the crate, he removed the panel above his head, placed it aside, then stood on his tiptoes, sticking his head through the humming hole.

The inside was dark and littered with clumps of dust and hair and dead flies. Mustiness was the predominant smell, with a trace of copper, like pennies, which he supposed could have been whatever alloy the duct was made from. But a slight salty tang prickled his nostrils. He flashed his Maglite into the gloom.

No droppings here, either.

Alvin twisted around on the balls of his feet to check the

other end of the pipe, and nearly jumped at the sight of a mottled purple fruit about the size of a watermelon, oozing clear slime from a smooth, intended gash.

The hole gurgled as more fluid oozed from it. Then it widened, exposing dozens of sharp little teeth. Its long body, at least a foot and a half wide, trailed down the shaft behind it, casting a shadow when his Maglite blasted white light on its eyeless face.

A lamprey? In an apartment building?

Whatever it was, Alvin wasn't about to stick around and find out. He ducked out of the duct so quickly the crate toppled below him, and he fell on his bony ass. The penis slithered through the shaft and dropped out of the vent, landing on him, its teeth gnashing.

Alvin caught it around the throat and hugged it, wrestling it like a gator, desperate to keep its mouth away from him. "Oh fuck! Oh fuck! Oh fuck!"

He rolled over the vicious thing, and if he didn't know better he'd have thought someone was pranking him with a robot movie replica of a giant floppy cock. But it was warm and fleshy, and it kept oozing the sticky clear fluid on his neck and face as he struggled, and he as he spit out a salty gob of it, the full weight of it stuck him like a dick slapped on his forehead.

It was *pre-cum*.

Alvin gagged.

The Juicy Girl stepped into the doorway and screamed, dropping her laundry in front of her on the cement floor.

"What?" Alvin said, struggling. "You never seen a grown man wrestle a giant pecker before?"

The girl's legs gave out, and Alvin took a moment to marvel at the sort of wobbly way she fell to the floor, like she was using an invisible hula hoop. The giant peckerhead jerked toward her as she hit the floor, and Alvin used the distraction to haul back and punch it. Its flesh was soft and clammy under his knuckles.

The pecker returned its attention to the struggle, foreskin fanning out like one of those screamy dinosaurs from *Jurassic Park* as it bared its fangs at Alvin.

Too bad it doesn't got any balls, he thought, gripping it around the throat—*Shaft? Whatever the fuck it is...*

He felt its lower half wrap around him before he could kick it away, and suddenly it began to squeeze, crushing his scrawny ribs. He gasped, his grip loosening from the pecker's throat. Its mouth opened impossibly wide, and the head darted at him, foreskin enveloping his head like an executioner's hood.

The last thing Alvin the Exterminator felt before he blacked out was those sharp little teeth grazing over his scalp.

Unfortunately, he regained consciousness a short time later with his flesh dissolving, his screams of agony muffled by the warm, thrumming insides of the giant mutant pecker.

His death was most assuredly not humane.

ZOEY OPENED the door to find Dan standing in the hall with a cooked chicken, a bottle of white, and a stack of DVDs.

"Movie night," he said with a boyish grin, and leaned in to kiss her.

She stepped aside to let him in, and he moved past toward the living room, where he planted himself on the couch. He set the food on the counter, the wine bottle on a coaster—he was learning—and the DVDs beside it.

Zoey went to the cupboard and got down two long-stemmed wine goblets. She held them crisscrossed in one hand while she grabbed the corkscrew, and brought them to the couch. The chicken smelled excellent, making her stomach rumble. "What did you bring?"

"Oh, just a handful of the greatest films in the history of moviedom," he said.

"Moviedom?"

He shrugged. "It's a work in progress."

She looked through them: *Aliens, Prometheus, Predator, Batman v Superman: The Director's Cut*. "I guess I'll go with the *Alien* one," she said with little enthusiasm.

"Actually, it's *Alien* 2, not one. Excellent choice, though. Ripley is one of my favorite characters of all time. You'll love it."

Dan got up, and while he put the DVD into the player, Zoey poured the wine. He came back, drew an arm over her shoulder, and sipped his chardonnay.

They split up the chicken and rice, and ate on the couch while the movie played. A good way through, during what Dan had twice referred to as "the chestburster scene," a knock at the door interrupted them.

Dan paused the movie and glanced at his watch. "It's half past nine. Who the hell could it be?"

Zoey shrugged and got up. The movie was decent, but she wasn't really invested, too worried about her big meeting at work tomorrow to focus. "I'll check." She crossed to the front door and peered through the peephole. "It's Orson Ladd," she whispered to him.

"What does he want?" Dan asked.

Zoey addressed the peephole. "What do you want, Orson?"

"I need help," he said. He sounded frightened. "Something is wr-wrong with me."

She couldn't imagine why he'd want to talk to her, of all people. Aside from that day at the coffee shop—the same day Mr. Popadopolous had been found dead in the laundry room, having slipped in a puddle and landed on one of his tools, which had apparently penetrated his ear canal—she hadn't even seen him at all. Some of their neighbors had speculated he'd been sleeping during the day, waking at night only for casual encounters with women, possibly even prostitutes. There was talk at the last condo board meeting of having him ejected, but so far no one could think of an actual violation he'd made to any of the charter rules.

Still, the guilt gnawed at her for ditching him that night. "Orson, it's past nine. Can't we talk tomorrow? At the coffee shop?"

"It can't wait 'til tomorrow!" he shouted, his voice breaking.

"She has a guest!" Dan shouted back.

Zoey winced. "Orson, Dan's here. We're watching a movie."

Orson pounded feebly on the door once more. Zoey peered out, and saw that he stood with both fists pressed against it, eyes squeezed shut as if he was in immense physical or psychic pain.

Then his eyes snapped open, dark and full of terror, and he jerked his head to his left. He slipped away from the door, staggering off toward the stairwell, hands held out to protect himself. Zoey squinted at the convex lens, looking for any sign of someone out there in the hall with him, but unless the person was crawling on the carpet, it appeared to be empty.

She heard the stairwell door open. Then the red bell

alarm above her head went off, the sound drilling into her ears—*Like Mr. Popadopolous*, she thought—and she stepped away from the peephole, covering them.

She'd hated that sound ever since junior school, when someone had pulled the fire alarm right before recess, and they'd spent the entire fifteen minutes standing stupidly in lines of boys and girls when they should have been playing, and one of the boys had pulled faces at her from across the yard. Stuck in line, with Mrs. Winters watching the girls like a hawk, she hadn't been able to retaliate.

"What the hell?" Dan shouted, rising from the couch. "The bastard pulled the goddamn fire alarm! Right in the middle of the chestburster scene."

"Would you forget about the chestyburst thing?" Zoey said. "We have to leave the apartment!"

"It's not a fire! It's not even a drill!"

"We don't know he pulled the alarm..."

"Only one way to find out," Dan said, and moved past her to the door. He unlocked and unchained it, then opened it on an even louder rattling. He peered left and right before covering his ears and stepping out.

Zoey stood by the couch, watching the open door and the empty hall beyond, awaiting Dan's return.

The bell above the door kept jangling.

Dan stepped back into the doorway, startling her. "The alarm's been pulled." He turned to look down the opposite end of the hall. "Nothing to worry about," he said to Zoey's neighbors. "Some joker pulled the alarm." She heard a muffled reply. "I say, 'Some joker's pulled the alarm!' No, it wasn't me, you muppet. If it was me, why would I have said it? Go back to bed, for Pete's sake."

Dan stepped in and pulled the door closed behind himself.

"I tried to put the little handle thingy back, but it didn't work. Just have to wait it out, I guess." He peered out the peephole. "Cripes, they're still going. I told them it was a false alarm..."

"It's building policy. We should be going, too."

"Oh, Zo." He gave her a condescending pout. "Don't be so uptight, eh?"

"Maybe you should go home," she suggested, trying not to sound angry.

"I thought I was sleeping here tonight?" He winked. "Why do you think I got you all drunk and frightened?"

"I really wasn't in the mood tonight, anyway. And this—" She indicated the alarm, still being hammered by its clapper. "—this hasn't helped *get* me there."

"Orson Ladd strikes again," Dan said.

"What's that supposed to mean?"

"It means, he's been worming into your head for as long as I've known you. Messing with your mind. I *know* you still feel guilty about leaving him that night—"

"That's not fair..." she said, feeling small and ashamed. She slumped down on the couch, reaching for her glass of wine.

"He's playing on your sympathetic nature, don't you see? He knows you're a soft touch."

Something heavy fell against the outside of the door.

"Oh great! There he is again, right on time," Dan said, and twisted the door handle, jerking it open. "Right, I've had just about enough of—"

An enormous flesh-toned caterpillar rose up on its veiny belly, its purple head rearing back, its vertical, blood-red mouth opening wide. Dan stumbled back from the door, his voice rising in a scream of unadulterated terror as the creature vomited a thick, pearl-colored fluid onto him, and he held up his hands to shield himself from the violent onslaught, his scream ending in choking and gasps.

Zoey froze on the couch, unable to mentally process the sight of a giant penis spasming as it showered her boyfriend in sticky gobs of semen while the alarm still rattled above his head. It was like something out of a low-budget horror movie, only the penis creature was not a puppet, nor was it CGI. It was flesh and blood and jism, and it was standing in her doorway.

I have to do something...

Determined, Zoey grabbed the wine bottle, and thrust herself to her feet.

The penis had stopped spewing and slumped onto its belly in front of Dan, who dripped with its creamy filth, flicking his hands and spitting out a mouthful. Then the creature hunched up like an inchworm and dragged itself toward Dan, who sat in a very unfortunate position, with his legs splayed.

Zoey called his name, and he turned to her, looking confused and frightened. "Get out of the way!"

Dan drew his legs up and rolled to his side just as the creature's blunt, eyeless head began prodding the rug where he'd been sitting, like a blind man's cane. In the brief respite, Zoey launched the wine bottle, and it shattered on the creature's side. Its thin skin split open in several places, bleeding.

And they say pussies are fragile, Zoey thought.

The creature wobbled, seemingly stunned. She seized the opportunity to run for Dan. "Are you okay? It's not acid or anything, is it?"

He blinked painfully, wiping the milky fluid from his face. "No, it's just really fucking stinging my eyes!"

She grabbed his slimy hand, and hauled him to his feet.

"Where are we going?" he asked her, in a small voice reminiscent of a child's.

"To the balcony," she said, and he followed along behind her as she ran.

ORSON BOLTED UP seven flights of stairs, not daring to look down, fearing the beast was behind him, mere dick inches from his feet.

He never should have let it back into his apartment, he knew that now. He'd just been so overjoyed to have finally found it, after a long, desperate week without hope, that he hadn't been able to think straight. So he'd opened the door, and let the lonely, miserable thing crawl up under his bathrobe. It had fit like a glove against the open sore the surgeon had left for his eventual transplant, looking somewhat like a nasal cavity without the nose. Orson had closed the door gently, had locked it, and untied his robe to look down at himself.

"My beautiful prick," he'd said.

It had returned.

He'd washed it standing in the tub before the full-length mirror he'd had installed, admiring its heft and shape. The wound itself had mostly healed, the only evidence a small red-brown ring of scar tissue at the base of the shaft.

The prick itself had seemed larger somehow, and Orson hadn't questioned it at the time, just assumed it was an optical illusion caused by its absence. Now he knew better. It really *had* been growing—was *still* growing—because of the cancer inside it.

At the hospital, once he'd surfaced from unconsciousness, the surgeon had actually declared him lucky. Gina maiming him had saved him the trouble of going through chemotherapy, and the possible penectomy operation if chemo hadn't worked.

He would have gladly suffered months of radiation sickness, had he known the alternative.

When his prick hadn't been having its way with dozens of women over the past six weeks, returning to him nightly—God only knew where it spent its days—Orson had researched the symbiosis between parasites and their hosts. He'd read about the lancet liver fluke, a microorganism eaten by cows and humans, which laid eggs in their intestines. The eggs were excreted, eaten by snails, and the live flukes eaten again by ants. The fluke was so sophisticated in its programming that it was actually able, once it had burrowed into the brain of its ant host, to draw the ant to the top of a blade of grass to be eaten by cows, effectively committing suicide.

Orson found it humbling to know he was no more sophisticated than an ant.

In the meantime, he'd worried about his sperm. How many of those women had been on the pill? How many potential offspring did he now have growing inside their bellies? Or was his sperm even viable? Orson hoped to God it wasn't.

Meanwhile, his prick grew and grew. John Holmes would have been jealous.

Then, for an entire week, his prick hadn't visited him. He'd waited up, had even scheduled dates, but his dates had left unhappy, and Orson had drank himself to sleep. Seven days, feeling both hopeless and hope*ful*—wishing his prick would return while praying he'd never see it again.

And tonight, it came back.

As tall as a man and throbbing, leaving wet slime trails on his carpet, his prick had returned once more. Orson had taken one look at it and run terrified from the apartment, running to the only person in the building he'd thought might lend him a sympathetic ear: Zoey Esprit. She would help him if anyone would.

But she hadn't. Her posh British boy-toy had been there, and now Orson was running for his life, hurtling up the stairs two by two, hot breath tearing his lungs as his penis—a giant Freudian metaphor—chased him like something out of a childhood nightmare.

Orson burst through a door marked 23 and raced into the hall. He risked a glance behind himself as the door swung to a close, saw nothing lurking in the brightened stairwell, and carried on running.

His neighbors were leaving their apartments, heading his way. The fire alarm had drawn them from their slumber, or whatever they'd been doing. Most of them looked annoyed, but annoyed was a hell of a lot better than being dead.

Orson pushed through and hurried into his apartment, straight to the kitchen, and to the knife drawer. He took what he needed and returned to the door, catching a glimpse of himself in the foyer mirror. A madman in a bathrobe, holding an electric knife, hair damp with sweat and falling in his crazed eyes.

He hurried out, back to the stairs. A long line of aggravated people trudged slowly down to the first floor, the elevators stopped by the fire alarm. Orson buzzed the knife, startling the closest people to him.

A well-dressed Indian couple stepped aside with looks of undisguised terror.

"Out of the way! The dickless wonder's gone nuts!" some college bro shouted over the alarms, and his wonky-toothed girlfriend laughed at the play on words.

Orson zipped the cordless knife at him, and the kid fell back, bumping into the Indian couple behind him and dragging his girlfriend down by the hand. The way cleared then, as those in front looked up to see a lunatic in a bathrobe brandishing a weapon, and pressed themselves against the wall.

He bounded down the rest of the way, hoping he wasn't already too late to save Zoey and her boy-toy.

PRICK FELL into the sticky sludge of her own amniotic fluid, feeling the agony of loss for the millions of eggs crushed under her weight. Barely conscious, she lay there bleeding from her new flesh on her surviving brood, trying to muster up the will to carry on.

Prick blinked amnion from her eye and saw the bipedal not-so-giant female through a milky haze, dragging her companion out onto the balcony.

Prick burned with a single desire: the female had to pay.

She hunched up and dragged herself along the carpet, hunched and dragged.

In a moment, she would have them—both of them—close enough now to see the terror in their eyes. She would swallow them whole, digesting them over several hours as she had the exterminator, or immobilize them and eat them slowly, torturing them, savoring each bite.

Prick launched herself at the female, and slammed

against an invisible barrier. She fell back, stunned, writhed in pain on the floor.

The female laughed.

Prick twisted to face her enemy, seething with rage at the heavy glass separating her from lunch.

She rose groggily, threw herself at the glass.

Both meals drew back from the door, casting nervous glances over their shoulders.

On Prick's third attempt, the glass began to crack.

ZOEY AND DAN stepped away from the balcony door, and looked over the ledge. A jump of eight floors might not kill them, but it wouldn't be pleasant. Especially now that the grass was milling with people. It wasn't as if they could crowd surf.

"Help!" Zoey shouted, waving her hands. Dan joined her. Over the blaring alarms, no one heard them, or at least made any indication they had. Sirens had joined the cacophony, making it even less likely they'd be heard.

"We could try to climb down to the next balcony," Dan suggested, but he didn't sound enthused.

The creature threw itself against the door a fourth time, streaking the glass with blood, making Dan jump up close to her, smearing the thing's vomit or semen on her favorite blouse.

The crack spider-webbed outward.

Soon, the glass would shatter.

A choice had to be made: certain death at the mouth of this... *thing*, or climb down to the next balcony, risking the fall?

The creature drew back, its blood-red urethra—mouth? —*eye?*—widening, and hurtled itself at the glass.

The cracked glass warped outward, held firm by the sheet of clear plastic on the outside. One more strike and the tiny square shards would fall onto the balcony and the creature would be upon them.

Dan grasped her hand. Together they watched as the thing began to dance behind the cracks, jerking back and forth like a puppet dancing on its strings.

Blood spattered the inside of the glass.

Vaguely, over the sound of the alarm, Zoey heard whining, or drilling.

A whirring blade tore through the front of the giant penis under its purple head—the frenulum, she supposed—and gouged downward, spewing blood and meat and flesh at the glass. Its urethra unleashed a horrible screech—*Mouth it is*, Zoey thought—and it began to topple sideways, smearing its insides down the door like a bug on a windshield.

Orson stood behind it, holding a bloodied electric knife, his arms and face and bathrobe drenched in gore.

"I told you it couldn't wait," he said.

"Is it dead?" Dan asked.

"I don't know, but I'm not waiting around to find out." He pulled on the door. With the broken glass pushed outward, it wouldn't budge beyond the bulge. "I'm gonna find something to smash it."

Orson disappeared into the apartment.

"He'll probably end up rooting through your sex drawer," Dan said.

Zoey flashed him an angry look, and eyed the creature for movement. It appeared to be breathing, its body rising and falling so slightly it could have been her imagination.

A moment later, Orson came back with her bedside drawer.

"What did I tell you," Dan said.

Zoey just rolled her eyes.

"Step back," Orson said as he prepared to launch the drawer. Zoey and Dan pressed back as far against the ledge as they could, while below the fire engines finallly arrived, their red lights flashing over the pebbled exterior wall.

The drawer punched through the glass, landing on a corner and splintering, spilling her contact lens solution, glasses case, lubricant, condoms, her little pink vibrator, and other nighttime things onto the balcony.

Both men stared at the vibrator.

"What?" she said. "Everyone has a vibrator, it's perfectly normal!"

Orson shrugged. "I have a vibrator," he said, and when Dan gave him a look, he added, "Don't you judge me."

Zoey flashed them an angry look, scooped her vibrator up into the pocket of her loose pants, and stepped over the mess into the apartment.

"What the hell is that thing?" Zoey asked, quickly step-ping over the creature.

"That was my penis," Orson said.

She looked down at it from a cautious few steps away. "Why is it so..." There was no other way to describe it than, "...*huge*?"

"It's not *that* big," Dan scoffed, and jumped over the creature.

Orson looked his rival up and down. "What the hell happened to you?"

"I don't want to talk about it," Dan mumbled, swiping thick liquid from his shirt onto the carpet.

Zoey stopped suddenly on their way to the door, throwing her arms out wide to halt the men walking on either side of her. "Hang on a second," she said, turning back to the creature on the floor.

"What are you doing?" Dan asked.

"I'm gonna make sure that fucker's dead," she told him, approaching it cautiously.

The creature's body expanded and contracted, like the shallow breath of someone sleeping. She wondered, did it have organs? Lungs? A *brain*?

She would soon find out.

From the gaping wound Orson had carved with his turkey knife, she saw bits of bone: a ribcage, a spinal column. At first she thought it might be the creature's, that it had somehow *grown* a skeleton—which wasn't much crazier than the fact that Orson's severed penis had become sentient, and grown to the size of a human.

But as she drew nearer, she saw other bones among the gore of its innards: long with knobby ends, like human limbs, and smaller bones like fingers, and it dawned on her...

It had eaten someone alive.

Swallowing any pity that might have remained for the creature, she stepped down hard with her high heel on its bulbous head.

The men sucked in wincing breaths behind her.

"Oh grow up!" she said, wiping her shoe on the carpet.

Satisfied, she crossed the room to where Dan and Orson waited.

The kitchen faucet began to rumble and shake.

What now? she thought, glad her insurance would cover most of the damage to her apartment.

The three of them turned to each other, taking in one

another's confused and frightened faces, and a violent splash arose from the bathroom.

PRICK WAS DYING.

Killed by the hands of her God. God Orson. The Creator.

She lay on the carpet in a puddle of her own blood and shards of glass, while the female and male followed God Orson to the exit.

And then she felt it: tremors in the floor arising from the pipes and the ducts.

They were coming.

As the female's foot squelched down on her head, ending Prick's short life, she found some comfort to ease her journey through that last long, dark, warm and wet tunnel toward death.

Her children had come home.

THE FAUCET ROCKETED UP from the sink with a clang, smashing a hole in Zoey's ceiling.

Zoey turned to watch as hundreds of fat pink larvae oozed out of the pipes, crawling over each other, their purple heads searching blindly.

Not larvae, she thought. *Penises. Its brood. Her* babies.

A wary glance down the hall confirmed there were more of them spilling out of the toilet, splatting wetly on the bathroom tile, and from the slots of the air vents, and from the cold air return... They swarmed the chicken carcass, devouring scraps of meat and leftover food on the plates.

She shook Dan, who stood immobile, gaping in horror at the sight before them.

"We have to get out of here!" she shouted.

Orson threw a final glance toward his giant cock, and nodded defiantly. He lead the way into the hall. Zoey and Dan followed him. He jerked down the remaining fire alarm as he passed, and threw a look over his shoulder. "So everyone doesn't come piling back in," he explained.

It seemed smart to Zoey, but when Orson opened the door to the stairwell and began going up instead of down, she wondered if he'd lost his mind.

Maybe his brain really was in his penis, she thought with bitter amusement.

"Where are you going?" Dan asked. "We've got to get out of here."

"I'm not leaving," Orson said, and a drop of gore fell from the electric knife onto his slipper. "Not until all of those wriggly little fuckers are dead."

"But *how?*" Zoey wondered.

Orson smiled darkly. "I'm going to call them back to Papa," he said, and nodded toward the ascending flights. "Go. You don't want to see this."

"No," Zoey said. "I'm staying to help."

He shook his head. "This is my fight."

"But what if your plan doesn't work?"

"It'll work," Orson said. "And if it doesn't... well, hopefully Mrs. Bartleby calls in some good fumigators. Now go on." He flashed them a smile. "Make lots of babies."

Zoey and Dan exchanged a brief look—an identical "Is he nuts?" expression on their faces—and started down the stairs.

Orson watched them go, catching a good glimpse of the last great ass he'd ever see—the last *two* of them, if he was to be honest—and turned to climb the stairs.

Five minutes later, Orson sat on the couch in front of his television. He'd set a tube of strawberry-flavored lubricant and a box of Kleenex on the table beside him, and he flicked on the cable box to his favorite channel. On the screen, two porn stars he knew by name violently scissored each other, sharing a long purple dildo between them, crying out *"Fuck yeah! Fuck yeah!"*

The stirrings of arousal had always brought his penis home.

He hoped it would bring her babies.

SOPHIE AND DAN mingled into the crowd of sleepy, annoyed apartment-dwellers, the lights of two fire engines flashing red over their faces. Some gave them strange looks, but most didn't paid no attention as they stood waiting for the alarms to stop.

"I'd like to take this opportunity to apologize on behalf of my gender," Dan said.

Zoey laughed and shook her head. She took his hand, and he gave her a quizzical look. "Don't be a dick," she said.

The two of them smiled and looked up, way up, hoping like hell Orson knew what he was doing.

ORSON LADD SAT WATCHING the women punch each other's cervixes with lubed fists, and thought back on his life.

He'd slept with hundreds of women in his thirty-one years, but he'd never accomplished much else in his life. He'd gotten his real estate license, sold some condos and homes to young couples starting their lives together, and that was fine, it had been rewarding, but he'd mostly done it for the money. He'd learned how to play guitar, brew his own beer, played on a coed baseball team, taken salsa and cooking lessons, but every one of those pastimes had been to impress women.

Orson drank the last gulp of lethal brown sludge. Swallowing, he heard the first rumblings from the pipes below.

"This is it, Orson..."

A moment later, the toilet erupted. The kitchen faucet exploded under the pressure, sending a shower of miniature penises splattering against the cabinetry, the counters and the tiles. When the heat kicked on, they began pouring out of the vents until the screws snapped and the vent covers popped off, spilling out onto the floor, crawling over each other in a writhing mass that swished and undulated like a pink and purple ocean, its surf teeming with tiny penis-shaped piranhas as the apartment slowly filled.

Orson shook violently, painful spasms gripping his innards. He'd drank half a box of rat poison, unsure how much would be lethal, only certain he'd need to consume a lot of it if he wanted to kill them all.

The first wave climbed up to his shins, dozens of the little maggot-like creatures sticking to his hairy legs, nibbling his flesh, crawling upwards. As the swarm overtook him, he untied his bathrobe, let it fall to his sides, and spread his arms wide to let all of his bastard creations come unto him.

His entire life had been consumed by thoughts of pussy, but it was pricks that consumed him in the end.

As the last of them plopped bloated and dead from his picked-clean bones, the alarms finally stopped ringing.

NOTES: The idea for this story came from a joke between extreme horror author/director Matt Shaw and me. After the modest success of my novella *Woom*, we were spitballing— probably not the best choice of words, considering the subject—ideas for a project to co-author. Since we couldn't decide on anything, mostly because I'm a massive control freak, I pitched an idea for a story about a giant sentient penis that maybe eats people, loosely based on an old German comedy-horror movie called *Killer Condom*. Matt thought it was amusing, and I started writing it as an experiment, to see if I could still write comedic horror. Not sure it quite worked out, but nestled against Matt Shaw's *Hole*—so to speak—it seems to have entertained at least a handful of readers. Think of the mind that gave birth to it what you will.

THE PASSION OF THE ROBERTSONS

I don't know any stories I'd call a *genuine* Christmas miracle, but since you asked I'd have to say the closest was when Harry Maitland met Mr. and Mrs. Robertson on the closing shift at the Hometown Hardware a couple of years back.

You've heard of this so-called "war on Christmas"? Well Eric and Jean Robertson had been fighting that battle on the front lines before the lines had even been drawn. From the day after Thanksgiving until just after New Year's they'd led a shock and awe campaign of charity work, door-to-door caroling and chants of "Merry Christmas" to just about everyone they met. Not "Happy Holidays," oh no. Not *ever*. Eric and Jean were "put the Christ back in Christmas" types. If you said to them, "Happy Holidays," you'd get a thousand-yard stare and hear them mutter under their breath, reminding themselves to cross you off their "Nice" list for next year.

And God help you if you wished them a "Happy Hanukah."

These people ate, shat and slept Jesus—and not just on Sundays when Reverend Davies passed around the collection plate. So when an atheist stumbled into their midst on the day the lady's true love gave her three French hens and a partridge in a pear tree, that is to say December 28th, the Robertsons felt a little "Christmas cheer" was in order.

When they came across Harry at the hardware store, it was just about quitting time. Beer o'clock for Harry, if the last few customers didn't dawdle. It had already been a "day from Hell," as Harry himself might have called it in those days, and he wasn't about to stand for their Bible-thumpery.

Come 9:05 the Robertsons finally gathered up their purchases at the front counter, having ignored both announcements over the P.A. that the store was closing. Harry grudgingly scanned the nylon rope, the rolls of duct tape and plastic wrap... and he couldn't stand by and say nothing any longer.

"Got a hot night planned, huh?"

Mr. and Mrs. Robertson just blinked at him.

"It was a joke," Harry mumbled. "You know, because of the..." He shrugged, his humor having flown over their heads. "Never mind."

He rang up their odd purchase and said nothing further until the couple hit him with their standard "Merry Christmas."

"It's not Christmas, anymore," he snapped, and it was the worst possible thing he could have said in that moment. "It hasn't been Christmas for like three days."

Mr. and Mrs. Robertson eyed him with suspicion, as if he'd admitted he belonged to one of those strange religions that handles snakes, or worships their ancestors. They snatched their bag from Harry's hand and stormed out into the snow.

"Have a good night," Harry called after them with heavy sarcasm. He'd already begun to count his till as the door swung shut.

At 9:38 Harry finally locked the front door and drew the security cage shut. As he crossed to the bike racks he spotted a station wagon sat at the far end of the darkened, otherwise empty lot, someone parked illegally overnight. If he'd noticed it before he'd closed the shop he might have called the cops and had it towed.

It was too late for that now. Harry had bigger fish to fry. A good few inches of snow had come down since he'd biked to work and he'd need to walk it across town to the Ram's Head here. After the day he'd had the call of the drink was strong. He'd planned to down a few shots with Marianne, his favorite bartender—she quit a few weeks after the incident in question, fancied herself an actress—before he got down to the good stuff.

Harry liked the dark beers, the kind so thick they were practically meals in a glass. Just perfect for when you hadn't eaten anything since lunch and also had an urge to get plastered. A beer like that fit the bill most days for Harry Maitland. The hardware store didn't pay him well enough to support both dinner takeout and his after-work proclivities, and he'd never been the kind of guy to brown-bag it.

Crouching in the dark beneath the busted streetlamp, Harry slipped a hand into his jeans pocket for the keys to his bike lock. He fumbled them out and jabbed one of the duplicates blindly for the keyhole.

That's not iiiit, he thought, mimicking the way his latest ex-girlfriend had teased him in singsong while he fumbled under the sheets.

Harry might have laughed it the sound of tires squealed hadn't startled him.

He dropped the keys on the ground and spent a tense moment sifting through the snow in the dark before he noticed the bike racks and the brick wall behind them had brightened considerably and were *still* brightening while he fumbled.

When he finally clued in that a car was speeding toward him, curiosity had him spin around when he should have been diving out of its way.

Behind the windshield of the advancing station wagon Mr. and Mrs. Robertson sat with matching halos of dome light, ferocious determination in their eyes. A moment later the bright white of the headlamps blotted them out of Harry's sight.

When the rust-flecked grill slammed into his pelvis, Harry saw nothing but black.

"—ON OUR NAUGHTY LIST," Harry heard Mrs. Robertson say as his world came back into sharp focus.

Under different circumstances waking to what he saw that night in the Robertsons's den might have filled him with nostalgia. The walls had been decked with tinsel and holly, stockings hung from the stone fireplace, a warming fire rumbling in the hearth. A plate of neatly iced gingerbreads and sugar cookies lay on a green-fringed table runner alongside a crystal dish filled with pinecones and fragrant potpourri, and three gold candles in polished silver sticks, one each—Harry suspected—for the Father, the Son and the Holy Ghost. A brass version of "Joy to the World" crackled from a record player while Mr. and Mrs. Robertson sat Indian-fashion on the carpet wrapping gifts and placing them under a gargantuan plastic tree held upright by a wire nailed to the wall near the ceiling. The plastic angel stood askew on the crown of the tree, its tiny hands clasped in prayer.

It was almost like Harry had fallen asleep on Christmas Eve during *It's a Wonderful Life* and woke to discover his parents hadn't put him to bed and he could watch—if he pretended to still be asleep—as they placed gifts from Saint Nicolas under the PVC tree.

Except for the pain, that is. The pain wouldn't let him wax nostalgic.

Struggling to move his limbs, Harry tried to look down but something constricted his head at the neck. A hazy memory recurred of Mr. Robertson slapping a roll of duct tape down onto the counter and finally Harry became truly horrified at his predicament.

"What is this? Why can't I move?"

Looking over his shoulder, Mr. Robertson stood abruptly, appearing both anxious and pleased, dressed in a ridiculous Christmas sweater with a shirt collar peeking out above the neckline. The man smiled. "You're awake. Welcome to our humble abode."

Looking like she'd just stepped out of a '50s television show in a checkered button-up dress with beige nylons, pearls and a plain white apron Mrs. Robertson plucked up a crystal goblet and a decanter filled with a creamy yellow-white liquid from the coffee table. "Would you care for some egg nog?"

"No, I don't want—" Harry remembered civility wasn't required of him. *"What are you doing to me?"*

Jean Robertson set down the decanter and offered him a pitying smile. "Relax, Mr. Maitland. You've been heavily sedated but you are very badly injured. Struggling wouldn't be in your best interest."

Eric gave his wife a look of concern. "Do you think I hit him too hard?"

Her response was curt. "He'll be fine."

"What if he's paralyzed?"

"He's not *paralyzed*, Eric. Are you paralyzed, Mr. Maitland?"

"I don't—" Harry swallowed a dry lump. "Why are you doing this to me?"

"Do you believe in God?"

Harry laughed in spite of his circumstances. Couldn't help himself, really. *"That's* what this is about? You fucking whackos—"

Mrs. Robertson slipped a delicate hand into the pocket of her apron and pulled out a dull black revolver. "Tut tut, Mr. Maitland. God is listening."

"Yeah? Well, God can *suck my fucking dick!"*

Pulling a face like he'd just sucked on a lemon, Mr. Robertson put a comforting hand on his wife's shoulder. Mrs. Robertson's naked lips rose in a sneer of disgust as she pointed the pistol at Harry.

"I don't *want* to shoot you, Mr. Maitland," she said. "But I cannot allow you to say such hurtful things about our Lord and Savior in this house."

Mr. Robertson dropped his hand to his side. "He's never going to believe, Jean."

"He'll *believe*, Eric. Did Thomas not believe when Jesus let him touch His wound?"

"What the fuck is going on here?" Harry demanded of his hosts.

"I'm glad you asked." Mrs. Robertson smiled like a teacher toward an attentive student. "Eric and I came to the realization many years ago that a man such as yourself—an *atheist*—would never truly appreciate the pain Jesus suffered *for our sins* . . . without suffering yourself. And you *will* suffer here tonight, Mr. Maitland. You'll suffer greatly."

The carol ended and the needle rose from the record.

Harry screamed to fill the silence.

Without missing a beat Mrs. Robertson fired the revolver at the ceiling. The bullet gouged a hole in the stucco above Harry's head and a sprinkle of plaster dust fell like snow on his face and chest.

"No one can hear you," Mr. Robertson said, slipping the old 78 back into its jacket. "Our closest neighbor is half a mile as the crow flies."

"It's just the three of us and God now," Mrs. Robertson agreed with a solemn nod. "And if He ignored the cries of His only begotten Son, I very much doubt He'll intervene for you. The next one's going in your chest," she added almost incidentally.

Harry had no doubt of the woman's sincerity. These people were lunatics. They were cuckoo for Christ. And if all they wanted was for him to believe in their Angry Man in the Sky, he had no qualms humoring them to save his own apostate ass.

No heretics would be burned at the stake tonight.

"Okay," Harry said, trying his damnedest to sound calmed. "Okay, you got me. I've just been pretending, okay?"

He blinked a drop of sweat from his eye. "I *love* Jesus. Jesus is *my dude*, okay? Can I go now? That's what you want, right?"

A new record started with a fanfare of trumpets and cavalry drums. The chorus sang "Onward Christian Soldiers," and Mr. Robertson returned to his wife's side. They took each other by the hand and smiled beatifically down on Harry.

"Jesus Christ," Harry breathed, his teeth beginning to chatter. "You people are *insane*."

Mr. Robertson approached the chair and tore the tape off Harry's neck.

Harry screamed again. The first three layers of skin felt like they'd come off with the tape and he wouldn't be surprised to discover he was bleeding.

The pain cleared and he peered down at himself, at his hands taped around several times to the dark, rich wood arms of what looked like an antique chair to Harry's untrained eye, with plush red fabric and buttons. He figured if he couldn't break the tape he might be able to bust the chair itself.

But only if Mrs. Robertson was unarmed.

When he saw what lay to the left of the coffee table and the sofa under its clear plastic cover, all hope of escape blew away like chaff before the wind, and Harry began to shiver uncontrollably.

Two four-by-four inch slabs of pressure-treated lumber lay on the carpet by the supper table, fastened together to form a crude crucifix. At the foot of it were a mallet and railroad spikes, along with two lengths of bristly rope.

And even though Harry was an atheist, he had watched the torture scenes from *The Passion* on the internet.

He knew what came next.

"The people walking in darkness will see a great light,"

Mrs. Robertson said reverentially, gripping the pistol in both hands against her chest, like a holy man clutching the Good Book.

Mr. Robertson crossed to the hearth and drew an iron poker from the tool rack. He hefted its weight as he returned to Harry's side.

"Unfortunately we'll have to forgo the traditional flogging of Roman crucifixions," the man said, moving around behind Harry. "We wanted your experience to be as authentic as possible, but obviously we couldn't go into one of those *awful stores—*"

Mrs. Robertson shook her head, glaring at the floor.

"—and we couldn't have the postman thinking we'd ordered smut online," Mr. Robertson continued gravely. "So . . . we'll have to make due."

"No!" Harry cried, jerking forward, desperate to evade the man's reach. "You can't do this to me! Turn the other cheek! That's what Jesus said, isn't it? *Isn't it?*"

He searched the woman's eyes for mercy. Mrs. Robertson afforded Harry another pitying smile, and the poker came down across his back.

Cold hard metal slashed through skin and cracked the bone beneath. Harry's scream tore his throat raw, the taste of blood causing his stomach to rebel. When the pain finally lessened he found himself thanking God Mr. Robertson hadn't stuck the poker in the fire to heat it up, and the realization of what he'd done struck him as deeply as the poker had sunk into his flesh.

"I get it now!" Harry screamed as a chorus of horns filled the room. "No atheists in foxholes! That's what this is, right? Well, you win! Glory glory Hallelujah, I *believe!*" he shouted, and he would have thrown his hands toward the heavens in fraudulent jubilation had they not been taped to the chair.

The corners of Mrs. Robertson's smile turned down in doubt.

"I told you, Jean," Mr. Robertson said.

Harry twisted round as far as he could. "Shut the fuck up, Eric. You want me to pray? I'll pray. Please . . ." He imitated a booming parody of a preacher's voice. "*God, please . . .* forgive my wicked ways! Spare me from the rod of your righteous followers! I know not what I do, you see? I know that now!"

Mrs. Robertson nodded toward her husband.

Harry heard the whoosh of the poker a heartbeat before it cracked against his ribs. The air catapulted from his lungs and he hunched over himself, weeping and whimpering, an itchy stream of blood trickling onto his thighs.

"Please . . ." Every breath felt like a spear stabbing his lungs. ". . . I'm begging you, *please stop this.*"

"'He who began a good work in you will bring it to completion at the day of Jesus Christ,'" Mrs. Robertson said, and she nodded to her husband again.

"What does that mean?" Harry cried. "I don't even know what that—"

The poker came down across his fully exposed back, the pain so omnipresent he puked up chunks of chicken fingers and French fries undigested from lunch.

"Why won't you *stop?*"

"You still don't understand, Mr. Maitland," the woman said with a shake of her head. "We're not doing this to hurt you. We're doing this to *save* you."

Harry wept.

Mr. Robertson struck him three more times before Harry lost consciousness.

Thank goodness for small mercies.

WHEN HIS EYES opened again Harry was lying on his back. Even through the pain he could tell they had spread him out on the makeshift crucifix. A choir pa-rum-pa-pum-pummed "The Little Drummer Boy" on the record player, and Mr. Robertson was on his knees tying Harry's left wrist to the horizontal board. Harry realized he couldn't move his arms even if they hadn't been tied down. He wasn't sure if it was the sedative or the injuries to his pelvis and back that had made movement below the neck impossible, but what he did know was that his hosts meant to drive nails into his hands and feet, and let him hang from their homemade cross until he was dead.

There would be no pleading with them. If there was one thing Harry had faith in, it was that. These two lunatics would not relent. He saw no mercy in their eyes, only the fervor of old-time religion.

The Passion of the Robertsons, he thought.

Blood trickled from the corners of Harry's lips when he laughed.

Eric Robertson gave Harry a queer look while picking up the mallet and spikes. With the tools in hand the man looked up at his wife. From his expression Harry could not tell if the look was for encouragement or in the hope she'd put a stop to this madness before it went so far they couldn't turn back. Mrs. Robertson was out of Harry's line of vision. But he didn't need to see her to know she'd nodded once more.

Mr. Robertson rested the narrow end of the spike on the meat of Harry's left palm, and poised the mallet above it to strike.

The sound rang in Harry's ears like the clang of a choir bell. Metal split flesh and separated bones like the parting of the Red Sea. Harry's agonized scream unintentionally harmonized with the choir of voices from the record player. Mr. Robertson muttered along to the music, and when he struck the spike again it was synchronous with the "ding" of their bell.

Harry had naively assumed the second strike would be less painful. It was not. The wrist contains eight bones, and each one detached further as the spike drove in, stretching outward so that his hand felt as though it might burst at the sides.

On the third strike, Robertson bashed his own thumb.

With a wincing intake of breath, the man brought his injured digit to his mouth and sucked on it. Harry managed a weak laugh through his tears.

"Give me that, you big baby," Mrs. Robertson snapped, as if she were talking to a child.

Through a blur of tears Harry watched Mrs. Robertson kneel at his side and snatch the mallet from her husband. He caught a glimpse of beige satin panties between her thighs and in some distant, painless galaxy Harry felt the stirrings of arousal.

The Last Temptation of Harry, he thought. *God, I really am going to Hell.*

Mrs. Robertson caught his eye and clucked her tongue in disapproval. But she wasted no time in scrounging up the other spike by tugging down her dress.

And while she drove the final nail, the pain blistering up

his arm with each additional strike, Harry focused what little consciousness remained to him on the shimmering fabric between her legs, imagining himself hammering railroad spikes into the delicate, downy folds of her privates, before crushing her husband's testicles with the mallet.

When the job was done, and the choir sang "God Rest Ye Merry, Gentlemen," Mr. and Mrs. Robertson hoisted the crossbeam onto their shoulders and dragged Harry and his crucifix toward the kitchen doorway, where they laid it to rest against the arch.

And so it came to pass that Harry Maitland, atheist, bad boyfriend, Hometown Hardware employee and part-time alcoholic, was crucified in the year of our Lord 2015.

Hanging by his hands, his lungs felt constricted. He could barely get a breath. Blood oozed from his stigmata and pattered on the carpet. They'd made him a footrest, but it was of little comfort or joy.

He would not repent.

He would not accept Jesus as his Lord and personal Savior.

He would *not* let the Robertsons beat him.

Looking up at their handiwork with smiles of approval, the Robertsons took each other's hands, and though his agony reigned supreme Harry wondered if their little passion play had ever been an attempt to save his admittedly wretched soul, or if it had been an excuse from the very beginning for the couple to torture a man to his death.

As they watched their sacrificial lamb for signs he'd received the Holy Spirit, Harry found himself studying the angel atop the Christmas tree, placed at an odd angle, and thinking about how the words *angle* and *angel* were similar, wondering if the similarity held a deeper meaning.

He noticed the top of the tree had bent at the same angle, the wire pulled taut.

"You forgot . . . the crown of thorns," he gasped, and chuckled when the Christmas cheer dropped from their holier than thou faces.

A discordant twang interrupted "Silent Night." A heartbeat later a small metallic object struck the wall behind Harry's head and the tree sprang forward, launching the angel through the air. Bulbs and ornaments crashed to the floor.

And like Harry had turned toward his inevitable destruction rather than leap out of the way of approaching death, the Robertsons whipped round as the tree landed in the hearth and burst into flames.

Mrs. Robertson's nylons caught next. She dropped to the carpet and began to roll but the fire spread to her dress, the carpet, the red and green table runner, while Mr. Robertson stared down in horror, seemingly immobile.

The fire alarm began to blare as Mrs. Robertson writhed on the carpet. Bulbs burst like popcorn. Ornaments and plastic needles dripped into a black puddle on the floor. The record had warped, the choral voices rum-pa-pum-pumming became ghostly and surreal.

Already the sulfurous smell of Mrs. Robertson's burning hair filled Harry's nostrils. Her cooking flesh smelled something like burnt pork and the coppery tang of bubbling blood. This combined with the foul stench of burning plastic should have conspired to make Harry sick.

Instead he smiled.

Calm as can be, Mr. Robertson bent to pick up the revolver from the coffee table. He turned his back but Harry could still hear the man ask God for forgiveness before firing a single shot into his wife's head.

The woman stopped moving.

Mr. Robertson's arm rose and he put the pistol in his own mouth.

Realizing he was in direct line of fire should the bullet pass through Mr. Robertson's skull, Harry tried to move his head. He could not, and so he closed his eyes instead, awaiting the end.

The second shot rang out. Hot blood struck Harry's face like a splash of holy water on a newborn babe. He heard the thump of Mr. Robertson's body hitting the floor. Unable to believe he'd survived, when he finally dared to open his eyes the fire had already begun to smolder.

Mr. and Mrs. Robertson were dead. Or if not dead, well done.

He was *saved*.

Saved by a nail.

And he had to wonder if it was a coincidence that nails had very near killed him, but a single nail had spared his life.

Now you won't see Harry Maitland around the Ram's Head these days. Harry doesn't come in here anymore, not since he found God that night at the Robertsons's house.

The fire alarms were tied to the Robertsons's home monitoring system, you see. When the voice of the customer service agent called over the box Harry thought he was hearing the voice of God. It was not God, it was a man named Jim from AlarmSquad Home Security.

Now I have to ask you, do you think what happened to

Harry Maitland on the night of December 28th 2015 was an accident of fate? Or was it "divine intervention"?

Would you call that a "Christmas miracle"?

Heck, don't ask me.

But you have to think, if God was there to save him, then didn't God also let the Robertsons kidnap him in the first place? And if a god would put someone through so much torture just to teach them a lesson, then what the hell kind of sick, depraved sadist have we been praying to all these years?

Not any kind of god I'd want to stand before awaiting judgment, that's for damn sure.

NOTES: In the summer of 2017, after having just released my second horror collection, *Video Nasties*, I was tasked to write two new "extreme" horror stories for upcoming anthologies. This story was originally published by Splatterpunk Zine's Jack Bantry in *Splatterpunk Fighting Back*, edited by Kit Power (*Godbomb!*). The other ("The Boats") was published in *VS:X*, an extreme horror competition.

As an atheist myself (although not "practicing"), I've always had a keen interest in religious zealotry and the Catholic obsession with the Passion. I thought it might be fun to bring the two together for a Christmas "miracle." Anyway, if you feel I've been a little too hard on Christianity as some reviewers apparently did, and you're looking for a different take, my first novel *Salvage* plays it a little more fairly.

THE BURDEN

Amelia washed her father's trembling hands with a damp cloth, wrung it out into the bowl of cool water she'd set beside his wheelchair, and wiped sweat from his brow.

His sweat was not from exertion but from the heat in his upstairs bedroom. Her father never exerted himself anymore, and they had yet to begin their daily routine. Since Amelia had returned home to take care of him he existed in one of two states: sitting and resting. Sometimes she sat him in front of his bedroom window. Other times she sat him at the kitchen table or the back porch with a view of the bird feeders and the large maple her mother and father had planted when they'd bought the house several years before Amelia was born.

When she crouched beside him she could never tell if he saw exactly what she did. He could no longer communicate, except through simple eye movements, blinking once for *yes* and two for *no*. He couldn't feed himself, so he "ate" via an endoscopic tube. Couldn't bathe himself. Dress himself.

Couldn't go to the bathroom without her help. She would often find she was already too late.

Not long ago her father had been strong, healthy, active. He'd eaten right. Hadn't smoked, never drank to excess. When her mother had been with them (*God rest her*, Amelia thought reflexively, though she no longer believed in God), her parents had hiked the nearby woods each morning after breakfast, and biked the dirt roads to and from the house at dusk. He'd exercised his minds as well as his body, completing puzzles, reading mystery novels, making wood-working projects by hand.

James Adam Corbel had done everything experts had suggested to stave off disease, dementia and the eventual wasting away of old age. And like a hijacked jet, amyotrophic lateral sclerosis had crashed into his body and demolished all of his progress. Medical experts called his current condition "locked-in," meaning her father was locked inside of his own mind.

Amelia placed the modified Brain-Computer Interface on her father's head and booted up her laptop. The software worked using subdural implants, converting electrical impulses from the limbic system to interact via transmitter with software on the computer. Researchers had already used the technology successfully to help ALS patients communicate with caregivers and loved ones but after months of daily attempts her father had yet to respond.

She'd known the process would take time. In the original study it had taken weeks for patients to type out a single letter using BCI technology, and those results had been far better than previous attempts with locked-in patients. As far back as 1995, a journalist had written an entire book by blinking it to a transcriber. It had taken ten months and *two-*

hundred thousand blinks, at an average of one word every two minutes, to finish the book.

Amelia had taken a sabbatical from her duties at the Academy. She had all the time in the world to work with her father. What she couldn't count on was how much time her father had left to live.

Just one letter and she would consider the day well spent.

"Come on, Dad... Let's make today a good one."

The software launched on her laptop, a combination word processor and image manipulation program she'd "borrowed" from the Academy. The cursor blinked on the white page. On the opposite side of the screen was a three-dimensional wireframe ball.

The idea was that her father could either type a word or move the ball, depending on his mood or mental landscape. Her thought was that just using a word processor might be too restricting. This way her father could work at his own level. She wondered though, if giving him too many choices had been the wrong way to go.

"How are you feeling today, Dad?"

His moist, jaundiced eyes twitched toward her. He blinked hard.

One for *yes*. Not exactly the response she was hoping for.

"Can you type it for me?"

He merely looked at her.

"Can you move the ball?"

The wireframe ball did not move.

Eventually he blinked, but she suspected it was involuntary.

Weeks of this.

Sweat had broken on his brow again. She dipped the washcloth and wiped it away.

"Not too much longer now, Dad. I'll take you downstairs to sit at the window when we're done. I think I saw the cardinal out there earlier."

He blinked.

The eyes themselves expressed no emotion. No sign of whether or not he wanted to continue, if he was finished with today's attempt or if he was done with the research altogether. He'd never given expressed permission to participate, aside from a blink for *yes*. For all she knew the whole process was torture to him—from the minor surgery to insert the subdural implants to the daily barrage of questions.

His body was already a prison, and his facial expression did seem to indicate anguish. The upward arch of his eyebrows and his angled, twisted lips made Helena, the caregiver who came in daily to help, once comment that it looked like he was perpetually going to the toilet.

It could have been far worse. At least he could still blink. Some patients couldn't even control that. Without her father's blinks for *yes* and *no* she might have given up on the experiment entirely. She might have put him in a hospital. Let him waste away to nothing.

Tears prickled her sinuses and she held them back, not wanting to cry in front of her dad, who couldn't help but cry in response despite his once-rugged exterior.

If only she could tell what he was thinking, but that was something she also hoped to achieve. Not only did she wish to communicate with her father, over time she hoped other researchers might be able to use similar the technology to map the human brain and bridge the gap between humans and AI.

Without the constraints of language and movement, Amelia saw virtually no limit to how much Humanity could achieve.

Without the burden of the body restricting the intellect.

But right now she couldn't even get him to push a goddamn ball or type a single letter.

"Just... push the ball, okay, Dad?"

The ball remained still.

"Can you push the ball? *Dad?*"

Blink blink.

She brought a fist down hard on the small table. *"Can you please push the goddamn ball?"*

The laptop rattled. Something thudded to the floor downstairs.

Amelia turned to the doorway and the stairwell beyond, thinking she must have shaken something loose.

Don't know my own strength.

She leaned down to stroke her father's wispy silvery hair and kissed his clammy liver-spotted forehead. "I'm sorry, Dad. I didn't mean to get mad. I'll be right back, okay? Then I'll bring you down to watch the birds."

Her father didn't blink.

Amelia left the room. The stairs of the old house creaked as she descended. Her great-grandfather's grandfather clock ticked away in the empty foyer. As she reached the first floor she could see into the living room. From where she stood at the bottom of the stairs nothing appeared to be out of place.

"Good morning, Ms. Amelia," Helena said behind her.

Amelia jumped, not expecting the caregiver to arrive for another hour. The woman held bags of groceries in her hands and must have let herself in from the garage with her spare key. Amelia helped the young woman, pleasingly plump in her pale blue nurse's scrubs, to unload the food into the fridge.

Later she brought her father downstairs on the chairlift and while he stared out the window at the birds fluttering around the feeders and the stone birdbath under the big maple she sat in the old wicker rocker beside him catching up on some research on the role endocannabinoids played on pathological anxiety.

Amelia's main field of study was cognitive science. She'd worked through her doctorate and had moved into the research field upon graduating. After nearly ten years she'd decided practically begging for grants was something she no longer wanted from life, and had taken an open position teaching specialized cognitive biology at the Academy of Modern Science in Boston.

When her father had called about his diagnosis she'd packed up at the Academy within the week and taken the train home to Toronto. The trip had taken her nearly a full day, and on the way she'd wondered how a university professor with no children and no nursing experience was going to take care of a man who'd responded to her scraped knees as a child with a brisk *Walk it off*.

When she'd arrived home her father had already been using a walker to get around. His limbs had shaken uncontrollably and his fingers had curled up into virtually useless fists. He'd fibbed about the progress of his illness. His specialist had given him between two and five years to live, but likely no more than three.

That was six months ago.

Amelia closed her computer and turned to him. Outside the cardinal was back, a bright red male with a crest on its head. It landed in the birdbath, startling the sparrows, and splashed its wings in the water.

It used to make her smile to see the joy those simple creatures brought to him, this old fashioned "man's man" who'd wanted a son but had been equally happy—if not more—with a girl. Who'd taught her how to hook a worm, play baseball, fight back against bullies, and never let a man treat her like a second-class citizen.

With his face twisted in an eternal rictus it was impossible to tell if the birds still made him happy. Was there joy in his tired green eyes? She couldn't tell. His disease had advanced so rapidly in the past six months he could no longer utter even a single laugh.

Amelia rolled her father into the kitchen. After dinner— Helena had prepared the blend of fruits and vegetables and nuts for her father's endoscopic meal—Amelia helped Helena clean up and wash dishes.

On her way upstairs she leaned into the living room and saw the baseball lying in the middle of the wooden floor.

"Helena?"

The woman came in from the kitchen, soap foam crackling on her yellow plastic gloves. "Yes, Ms. Amelia?"

"Did you dust my father's baseball?"

The woman gave her a confused look.

Amelia tried not to sound upset as she pointed at the ball on the floor. "That's his Jackie Mitchell baseball. It's a collector's item."

Helena shrugged. "I didn't dust today, Ms. Amelia."

Amelia watched the woman head back to the kitchen before bending to pick up the ball. She turned it over in her hand, reading the signature, chuckling bitterly at the irony.

Her father had gotten it when Amelia was young to

remind her not to limit herself because of how the world might view her, that she could do anything she put her mind to with determination and strength. Jackie Mitchell had proved that by becoming one of the first female pitchers in professional baseball, and as her signature on the ball said she had beaten two legendary heavy hitters.

I struck out Babe Ruth and Lou Gehrig, it read.

That her father had picked this baseball of all the signed balls he could have gotten felt somewhat eerie.

ALS had also struck out Lou Gehrig; the disease itself had once been named after him.

Amelia wasn't sure she believed Helena hadn't knocked it down off the mantle, but she couldn't imagine why the woman would lie about it. If she *hadn't* moved the ball it had somehow managed to pop up out of its clear Lucite box stand, fall to the floor and roll to the center of the room of its own volition.

What was more unbelievable? That sweet trustworthy Helena had told a small fib for the first time since Amelia had known her? Or that an inanimate object had defied the laws of physics?

With a troubled frown, Amelia returned the ball to its stand.

IT WAS time to face the truth, she decided: the experiment just wasn't working.

Despite all the coaxing over the past twenty-three weeks her father couldn't manage to type a single letter using the BCI, and she was beginning to fear they were better off when he was still just barely able to hold a pen, eking out two words a minute.

His health seemed to be deteriorating faster, as well. His crippled arms hung loose from his shoulders, lacking muscle, tired flesh sagging. Ribs clearly visible. Spine protruding like the back plates of a dinosaur. Sallow, sunken eyes. Teeth receding from his gums.

Dr. Jorgenson said her father wouldn't live much longer than six months in his current condition. He'd suggested she consider moving her father into a hospital for round-the-clock care.

Amelia had strongly opposed the idea.

The decision to keep him home was entirely selfish, she knew. Imagining her father wasting away in the hospital like her mother had after her stroke... she couldn't go through that again. Couldn't watch it happen to such a strong man as he'd been.

But the obsessive in her—a trait she'd gotten from her father—needed to continue their work here. She felt close to a breakthrough, in spite of all evidence to the contrary.

She knew they could always try communicating through eye movement, not through blinks but using the tracking software on her laptop. Her father might have taken to it quickly despite his misgivings but she didn't want him to get used to the ease of it.

By making the BCI his only method of communication she hoped it would force him to adapt or risk never speaking to his daughter again. Although she couldn't blame him if he chose the latter, after she'd treated him like a lab rat for so long.

"Come on, Dad." Amelia positioned the headset on his thinning scalp as her laptop fired up. "Today's the day, huh?"

She didn't believe a word of it.

Her modified interface converted several signals from the implants in her father's brain—EEG, iEEG, LFP, and other sensory input—into data her computer could process. It worked because the brain itself was essentially a computer, albeit far more complex than her laptop. With the addition of small implants on the medial prefrontal and medial posterior parietal cortexes, she hoped he might eventually be able to manipulate a 3-dimensional version of himself through self-recognition, a notion first attempted using virtual reality tech.

If only she could get him to type a single letter.

The air was sweltering in her father's room today. She brought a fan upstairs and set it in the window. It whirred distractingly as she sweated hunched over the computer but the cool breeze curbed her growing agitation.

After half an hour of watching him blink his bleary eyes she stood up.

"All right, Dad," she sighed, her spine popping as she stretched. "I guess we're done here."

As she moved to flick off the laptop the sound of the fan lowered in timbre, the blades slowing until they stopped altogether.

She bent to check the plug. It was loose but didn't appear to be the problem.

As she stood again she saw her father watching her in the big mirror on her mother's vanity. Off to his immediate left she saw the alarm clock no longer showed the time in its large red digital numbers.

"Power's out?"

Her father blinked once.

She put a comforting hand on his shoulder. "I'll be right back, okay, Dad?"

Leaving him in his wheelchair she hurried downstairs to check the electrical box. Helena wouldn't be in for another hour or so—her two young children had the day off school—and Amelia still retained a bit of childhood superstition about being alone in the big old empty family home despite having been back so long. She'd always felt that unease even more acutely in the basement, and although she wasn't imagining ghouls and beasties in every corner like she had as a child, the memory of her brief sojourns to the basement for a popsicle or an errand brought that childish fear back to the forefront of her brain.

The basement was bright enough she didn't require a flashlight. Sunlight streamed in through the two grimy windows on either side of the furnace with their view of the leaf-clogged cement wells. Even if it had been fully dark down here, what the eye couldn't see would have filled in by memory.

The mind is all-powerful, Amelia thought as she stepped off the creaky wood stairs, assaulted by smells, sights, sensations and memories. The smell of dust, wood and damp concrete. The drip of the washbasin faucet. The gurgle of the floor drain, a misplaced tennis ball nearby. Dust on her fingers from the stair railing. Rough wood of the stairs on her sock feet.

A computer couldn't process so much disparate information so quickly.

The burden of the body, she thought.

Cobwebs hung from the corners of the rafters, wood charred black in places by a fire that had happened long before the Corbels had moved in. As a little girl she'd often wondered if anyone had died in the fire but she'd never bothered to ask her parents or look into it herself. The walls were exposed down to the lath. The concrete cold on her sock feet as she crossed to the electrical box.

Her father had updated from fuses to circuit breakers when Amelia was young, worried the old knob and tube wiring might cause another house fire. She flicked the main switch down and back up.

As she did a blue tendril of electricity unfurled from the switch and as it struck her finger an image blossomed in her mind of her father lying upstairs in his bed. Not vague as if from memory or imagination but genuinely as though she were sitting right across from him. He was looking directly at her, though she realized she was not looking directly back at him but at his reflection in the vanity, made obvious by missing flecks of silver backing and the chip in the lower right corner Amelia herself had made when she'd tripped and fallen playing dress-up with her mother's jewelry.

It was almost as if she were *looking out through her father's eyes.*

In the mirror, her father blinked.

Yes.

The mirror cracked suddenly, fracturing his face down the middle. The pain of the shock finally reached her nerves and the vision disappeared as quickly as it had come, sending her reeling back from the electrical box.

Amelia fell down hard on her butt and her left hand struck the yellow-green tennis ball which rolled lazily toward the sports equipment bin.

Standing and rubbing her sore buttock, she wondered how to explain what had just happened. She'd never experienced anything like it before, never imagined anything with such clarity.

But it *was* her imagination, of that she was certain. It had to be.

Idly she surveyed the room. Her gaze fell on the tennis ball.

How did that get out of the bin?

Two weeks had passed since the incident with the Jackie Mitchell baseball, long enough that she'd forgotten about it until just then.

Was it possible the two were connected?

She recalled the vision of her father, blinking at her in the mirror.

Yes, Amelia.

Amelia crossed to the bin and picked up the tennis ball. She placed it carefully beside the drain where she'd found it when she'd first come down. Stood again and kept it under a watchful eye.

"Can you move the ball, Dad?"

The ball didn't even twitch.

"Dad? Move the ball for me, please."

Amelia stared at it. *Willed* it to move.

She was so focused on the ball the sudden buzz and rattle of the air conditioner firing up outside made her jump, and she laughed at herself as cool air began to hum through the duct above her head.

"You're a *scientist*, for God's sake. This is *ridiculous*."

She scooped up the ball, deposited it in the bin, and ascended the stairs.

Her father was still in his spot by the window when she returned to the bedroom he'd shared with her mother. He sat facing the mirror, unable to turn away from his reflection.

The chip was still there in the glass where her face had struck when she was eight, breaking in incisor. Otherwise the glass was unblemished, not cracked as it had been in her vision—or whatever it was that had happened to her in the basement.

Amelia didn't know what she would have done if the mirror *had* been broken.

Gone crazy, maybe, she thought, and the fan whirred by, prickling the flesh on her forearms and making her shiver.

Her father blinked.

———

"You really should get someone out there to cut the lawn, Ms. Amelia." Helena stood at the kitchen sink washing the equipment she used to feed Amelia's father through the endoscopic tube. "My cousin, he owns a landscaping business. I could get you a family discount."

Amelia looked out over her father's shoulder at the backyard and saw Helena was right. The grass was shin deep. With the heatwave they'd experienced the past few weeks she was surprised the lawn hadn't just dried up and blown away on the wind.

"Thank you, Helena. But I can do it myself. It'll be good stress relief."

An hour later she'd forgotten the lawn, and sat again beside her father in the hot bedroom with the fan whirring.

A high-pitched grunt outside the window caught her attention.

Scowling at the interruption she went to the window. Her father hadn't made any progress since the day the power had gone out so it wasn't as if she would be missing anything at the computer anyhow.

Down below a young boy crept through the tall grass, hunting something. The grunt must have been from when he'd jumped over the tall wooden fence. He wore a backwards ball cap and a ball glove on his right hand, reminding her of herself when she was young, aside from the boy's lack of ponytail.

"I'll be right back, okay, Dad?"

Blink.

She hurried down the stairs and into the kitchen. Looking out through the glass in the backdoor she saw the kid shaking his head in apparent incredulity. Amelia opened the door and stepped out onto the porch.

"Can I help you with something?"

The tanned, freckle-faced boy looked up with worry in his eyes. His expression softened when he saw she wasn't mad. "I hit the ball. O-over the fence." With trepidation he looked at the surrounding grass. "*What is this?*"

"What is what?"

The boy blinked. "There must be like *a hundred balls* back here."

Amelia shook her head. "What?"

"In the grass. I can't even figure out which one is mine. You got like a dog or something?"

Amelia stepped off the porch onto the lawn. Immediately she spotted three balls within spitting distance: a racquetball, a tennis ball, a Nerf ball.

She took two further steps and saw more, each one nestled in the tall grass. It appeared to have grown around several of them. Others had rolled there recently, the tracks still visible.

Orange rubber balls, chewed pet balls, nicked croquet balls, dirty gray softballs, scuffed hardballs, stress balls, golf balls, even a pool ball. A whole neighborhood worth of missing balls, all of them somehow ending up here, in the Corbel backyard, under the shade of the maple.

What is this? she thought, unintentionally mirroring the boy's words.

Amelia shaded her eyes to look up at her father's window. The room was too dim to see inside but she could sense him looking down at her, and in her mind's eye he blinked *yes*.

"Take them," she said, heading back to the house.

"W-which one?" the boy stammered.

"All of them!"

Upstairs her father sat exactly where she'd left him. "Did you move those balls out there, Dad?" He eyed her blankly. She hunkered down in front of him, gripping the arms of the wheelchair. Not meaning to do it so violently. *"Did you?"*

Blink.

"How are you doing this?" Amelia knew how stupid it sounded but she couldn't shake the idea.

Blink blink.

"No. You don't know?" She frowned and stood, looking down at him. His tired green eyes tracked her movement. "I need you to work with me here, Dad. If this is... if this is *doing something* to you, I need to know."

He blinked hard twice.

"Do you want to stop?

No.

"What then? Why won't you meet me halfway here, Dad?"

He turned his eyes to the right and Amelia followed his

gaze to the laptop. The screen had gone into sleep mode. Their reflections looked back from the glossy black plastic.

Her father had never liked computers. Never wanted to work learn how to use them, never written an email or used the Internet. A computer had run him out of his job at the factory. It was only natural he hadn't wanted to cooperate with her after having shunned the technology for so long.

Hand-craftsmanship, that's what you lose when robots start doing the job of men, he'd always said. *You wanna make something special you do it by hand.*

"It's the computer, isn't it?"

Yes.

"But how...?" She shook her head, realizing the question was useless. Occam's razor suggested her father must have unintentionally created some sort of energy field with the modified BCI, but with the amount of balls in the backyard the field would have had to be *enormous.*

It simply wasn't possible.

"This isn't possible, Dad." She shook her head, trying to convince herself. "This can't be happening."

He blinked once, hard.

Yes, Amelia.

"Okay." She began pacing the small room, mind racing. "Okay if it's real, Dad, maybe you can do something for me..."

Her gaze fell on the bookshelf. Stacked horizontally in front of her mother's old mystery novels were several crossword books. She brought one to the desk and opened it to where he'd clipped a pen as a bookmark before he'd lost the use of his hands. She removed it and flattened the fold, nearly set the pen down on the pages but hesitated at what she saw.

The puzzles on both sides were already filled in, a single word repeated over and over in the boxes.

Heart thudding in her temples she flipped through the book and found more of the same, every single box filled in with one of three letters.

Amelia held the book up for her father to see. "Did you do this?"

He didn't blink. Didn't need to.

He'd written the answer all over the pages:

E|S|Y|E   S|Y|E|S   Y|E|S|Y|E|S
Y|E|S|Y|E S|Y|E|S|Y|E|S|Y E|S|Y|E|S

She set the book down on the desk beside the laptop and the pen on top.

"*Show* me."

He merely looked at her, eyebrows turned up, mouth turned down in a grimace.

Amelia let out an exasperated groan and flopped down onto the bed, holding her temples as she tried to piece it all together. "It's a joke then, isn't it? You... I don't know... what did you do, Dad? Did you fill it all in when you could still hold the pen? Did you get someone to put all those balls out there in the yard? Are you *messing* with me, Dad? Is this a *prank*?"

She looked down the length of her body from where she lay in the center of the bed and saw her father blink twice.

"I can't *do* this anymore, Dad. I love you, but I can't." A tear rolled down her cheekbone into her ear. Her vision blurred, looking at the ceiling because she couldn't bear to look at him as she said it. "You know I have to put you in the hospital, right? I have a *job* to get back to. People *need* me."

Yes.

"Is that what you want?"

No.

"Then what? Why won't you *show* me?"

That same anguished expression met her query.

Amelia wiped her tears and pushed herself up and off the bed. She grabbed the puzzle book and the pen from the desk and slapped them down angrily on the shelf.

His eyes followed her in the mirror as she left the room without saying another word.

AMELIA COULDN'T SLEEP EVEN though she was exhausted. After giving up on her father she'd finally mowed the lawn with the push mower, stooping to pick up all the balls the kid hadn't taken when he left. Still her body wouldn't relax. Her nerves were set on edge. Limbs full of energy.

Energy field, she thought. *Ridiculous.*

Rain pattered on the window.

Outside, a storm raged. Inside, the house stood silent.

Like Dad, except in reverse.

Amelia had made a decision today, and tomorrow she would place the call to Dr. Jorgenson. It meant an end to her pathetic "research." An end to her time with her father in this old house, holding on to memories of a life that no longer existed. Dad had always said he'd wanted to die in this house he'd made special for his family with his own two hands, and instead he would wink out of existence in a hospital bed just like Mom had.

She rolled to her side and watched the rain drizzle down the glass he'd replaced when she'd hit a homerun through it at age ten.

So much of this house was a part of him. Her mother had

loved it just as much but had poured herself into the furniture, the wallpaper, the knickknacks and photographs. Her father had redone the upstairs walls when dry rot and mold ruined the lath and plaster. He'd replaced the ugly nicotine-stained stucco ceilings, built the kitchen cabinets by hand, remodeled the upstairs bathroom and added a second half bath on the first floor where there'd once been a closet.

This was his house more than it was anyone's.

The house *belonged* to her father. Her father *belonged* here, not in some hospital.

Lightning flashed, brightening the windowpane.

She counted Mississippis in her head, the way he'd taught her when she was little. Thunder rumbled after four. Less than a mile away.

Amelia rolled onto her back, closing her eyes, letting the pattering of rain lull her to sleep.

Lightning flashed over her eyelids.

One Mississippi. Two Mississippi. Three—

Noticing the blue light hadn't diminished Amelia opened her eyes and saw him standing at the foot of her bed.

No—*standing* wasn't the right word. He *floated*, several feet above the floor.

A man made entirely of light.

Not light. *Energy.* He was pure bright blue energy.

Like a spark. Like lightning.

Plasma, she thought.

Amelia stared at the plasma man until his bright silhouette had imprinted itself on her retinas. He stood—*floated*—near the foot of the bed with his feet stretched toward the floor and his hands held straight at his hips, palms out, like a diagram of the nervous system. White light traveled through each vein, every nerve ending crackling like static electricity.

She could see his heart pumping. See the light flooding his limbs and his brain.

Amelia sat up abruptly, gripping the sheet. *"Dad?"*

The plasma man blinked eyelids made of energy.

Then he winked away, casting her bedroom back into darkness.

She leaped out of bed and hurried for the hall, catching her toe on the doorjamb. Crying out she grasped her foot, squeezing it to dull the pain.

Eyes full of tears, as much from the sight of her father's transformation than the sudden injury, Amelia limped into the hallway.

By the time she reached his bedroom he was gone.

His body still lay under the tangled sheet, but the *essence* of him, the energy that made James Adam Corbel the man she called "Dad," had moved on.

Dispersed.

Glassy eyes stared at his own reflection in the mirror. When she followed his gaze she knew for certain he did not see what she did. He didn't see the mirror had split down the middle, fracturing his reflection just as it had in her vision.

The vision he'd *shown* her.

Her father's eyelids closed for the last time by her hand.

Amelia sat beside his body a long time, considering what she had accomplished.

What *he* had accomplished with her.

Whether through her modifications to the BCI technology, the sheer force of his will or some unknown spiritual method, her father had transcended his body, releasing himself from the burden of the physical world.

The first *plasma man*.

She would destroy the headset and purge all of the data

in the morning but for now Amelia curled up beside what was left of her father, and slept.

NOTES: This story was written for a charity anthology of "mad science" horror called *Dark Designs*. I wanted my story to stand out from the others and since I was privy to what would be published alongside mine (since I published it along with Thomas S. Flowers and Jeffery X. Martin), I ended up crafting something that was more darkly psychological and somber than I might normally have written. Whether it ended up a success, a complete failure or somewhere in between, I'll leave for you to decide.

WHERE THE MONSTERS LIVE

IT WAS RAINING the day I brought my daughter's CD player back to the sex offenders under the bridge, and everyone was in a crummy mood.

Miami's weather is a blessing to those of us living on the street—at least until the rainy season, those summer months when you've got to get a roof over your head that isn't just a doorway alcove or the underside of a bridge, or you'll be soaked to the skin in seconds. The day I'd decided to go back home for the first time in months, it had already been raining three days, and most of us were sure the sun would never come out again.

By then I'd narrowed my search for the Rabbit Man down to three suspects: Tony Walker, Alejandro Gonzalez, and Orville "Popcorn" Perry, the convicted pedophiles I'd been living with for the last three months. Not everyone in Bookville had committed the sort of vile crimes these men had. Some were rapists, others were molesters, but most had been stuck there for petty sexual assaults, hadn't even spent a day in jail but had been forced to register anyhow.

Forced out of their homes, into the shadows, and under the bridge.

Statutory cases, groping, sodomy. Some drunk guy caught pissing in public near a school yard. You could almost laugh at a creep who's exposed himself to old ladies, so long as one of them wasn't your grandmother or your great-aunt. It's sick, sure, but it doesn't physically *hurt* anyone.

Regardless of their crime's severity, lobbyist Ron Book's ordinance forced these men and women to live 2,500 feet from any school, park, or bus stop. Without violating parole or removing their ankle monitor and skipping town, the Tuttle Causeway and the Everglades were the only places left for a sex offender to live.

Ron Book's folly had pushed them underground and off the grid. Instead of making Miami safer, he'd made the city a thousand times more dangerous.

Walker, Gonzalez, and Popcorn Perry—these monsters had done hard time. Gonzalez liked little girls. Popcorn preferred boys, but he'd gotten arrested for trying to diddle one of the girls on his school bus route. He told us she had a short haircut and had yet to hit puberty, so it was easy enough to imagine her as a boy despite not having the parts. From my understanding, Walker was a pinch hitter.

None of these men had ever killed anyone as far as I knew, but together they'd strangled the souls of at least half a dozen children. What had sent me rushing home that morning was Gonzalez had told a story the night before about the rabbit he'd had as a boy, reminiscing about how soft its fur had been. I could easily imagine it reminding him of the silken hair of his victims.

To ingratiate myself to them early on, I'd told a lie about how I'd done two years in Alamosa County for assaulting my niece. Popcorn and Walker had wanted details, so I fed them details: said I'd been grooming her for years before I actually got up the courage to go through with it. That I'd babysat for my brother and his wife—in truth, I have no siblings, only in-laws—for months just working up the nerve to touch her.

With my theater background, I've played everything from Hamlet's oedipal interests to Titus's cannibalism, but the part of pedophile was by far the most loathsome—particularly in light of why I was there. Popcorn had wanted to know about her underwear, if it had "decals," which I took to mean prints. Walker hadn't even bothered to conceal the erection in his frayed jeans. But Gonzalez had just stared, open-mouthed.

Afterward, I'd excused myself for a piss and ended up being sick in the shadows behind one of the big pillars.

One of those men had raped my six-year-old baby girl.

One of them was going to pay.

I left camp early the day I returned home, walking a little over three hours to the house where I used to live. My feet hurt and my clothes ran with a hundred rivers of dirt, but I hoped it would be worth the trek. There was a method to the madness, as they say. Or so I'd thought then.

Marnie was just pulling out of the drive when I arrived, our little girl Nola in the backseat playing with a doll I didn't recognize, making it dance. Neither of my girls saw me hiding behind the sprawling gumbo limbo in the Garrisons' front yard as they drove past, the two of them smiling and singing. Tears clawed out from my eyes, seeing the both of them looking forward instead of back, the way I thought they ought to be looking, toward a life when all three of us were still together. Toward the past I'd left behind in pursuit of my singular goal, this burning obsession. I'd been gone a little over four months by then, and it wasn't as though I'd expected life to stay in a sort of freeze-frame with me out of the picture. Still, seeing them singing along to one of Nola's CDs, seemingly as happy as you please... it was a blow.

Once the car disappeared around the corner, I did what I could to smother the pain. I drew the hoodie up over my head and crossed to the house, looking both ways, skirting the garbage cans lined both sides of the street, glad the municipality hadn't changed trash pickup to another day while I was gone. If Marnie had re-keyed the locks, God forbid, I figured I could wait around and break a window when the truck came rumbling up the street. But I didn't need to wait. My key slid in effortlessly. Twisting it in the lock, I let out a sigh of relief.

The house was just like I remembered it, if a little messier. It smelled nice, like the lilac shampoo both Marnie and Nola apparently still used. It smelled *clean*. Even the hints of last night's dinner in the garbage—a spaghetti sauce starting to turn—smelled terrific. Smelled like *home*. Stink permeates homelessness: the smell of trash, the smell of dirty streets, of fire bins and piss and other people's body odor, the wet dog smell that saturates your clothes and bedding, the smell of rust and dirt and decay.

It felt good being back here. Felt right. I wanted to strip off my clothes and climb into the shower, wash off the layers of grime the rain hadn't been able to make a dent on. Wash off all the hell and scum I'd had to wade through to get to where I was now, with the Rabbit Man almost within my reach, and stretch out on the fresh clean sheets. To wait for Marnie to come home and tell her I'd been stupid, that I'd give it all up if only she'd let me stay.

Our bedroom was exactly the way I'd left it. If she'd

taken down the pictures of the two of us together, the trips we'd taken before we had Nola, our engagement and wedding and honeymoon photos, I might have paused to reflect on its meaning. That they were still right where they'd been when I left made me think I could still come back if I wanted, if I could just summon the courage to quit. To give up on death and allow life and love back into my heart.

Anger rushed into my veins, and I pushed these thoughts away. Useless speculation. The thoughts of a coward. I had to protect my family, and the only way I knew how to do it was by leaving them behind.

I headed for the closet.

The night before I left home, Marnie had been off at a parent-teacher conference, listening to "suggestions" from parents who seemed to believe their fourth-grade children weren't receiving an adequate learning experience. As part-time drama teacher at her school (and sometime screen-writer), I was exempt from such proceedings, and so Nola and I were home alone, which happened every so often. While Nola read her favorite book for the hundredth time, listening to her little CD player, I watched the Yankees get their asses fed to them with the sound turned off.

After a while I headed out to the garage, fed up with the lousy game and Nola's repetitive pop music. She'd always been curious about the music Marnie and I used to listen to when we were young, and so I hunted down a handful of mixed CDs I'd made in college, most of them for when we'd turned the overhead lights off and the Christmas lights strung up around her dorm room twinkled over the bed like stars.

I came back to the living room with the box and hunkered down in front of Nola. She scowled when I turned off her music, but when I showed her the words I'd written on that first CD, her eyes lit up and she tented her fingers in a devious manner reminiscent of her mother hamming it up over some cunning plan she'd devised to rope me into something I didn't want to do.

The first song was "Sweet Child O' Mine." Nola seemed to enjoy it, even though she said Axl Rose's voice was funny. After that were a couple of songs I don't recall—one-hit wonders, most likely. Then came "Sympathy for the Devil," and it wasn't long before Nola and I got to howling along with Mick Jagger—"Hoo hoooo! Hoo hoooo!" I skipped the Chili Peppers' "Under the Bridge" since it's about suicide or heroin—or both—and even though Nola had already been through more than most kids had by sixteen, she was still only six.

Near the end of the CD, Nola and I had nestled down on the rug with the ball game flickering unwatched on the TV. I'd been staring up at the ceiling with my arms behind my head while Nola talked about what she liked and disliked about each song, a running commentary that was amusing at first but then sort of droned on as I began to daydream about grabbing the Rabbit Man by the throat and feeling his trachea splinter between my fingers. The image made me smile.

The cops still hadn't caught him, the man who'd assaulted my child, my little Nola, and I'd been spending most of my waking hours daydreaming about choking a man in a bunny suit to death as if the whole thing was a joke when the truth was far more sinister. Even then, I'm sure some dark part of me knew I could never move beyond the blind hatred, beyond thoughts of bloody revenge. That the wound he'd opened in me would turn gangrenous. Deadly.

I'd found myself sympathizing with those hovering parents Marnie and I used to berate. I heard the truth in meaningless catchphrases like "stranger danger." Buffer zones like Ron Book's sex offender ordinances, barring perverts and pedophiles from living within a short distance of any place children gather, seemed to make some kind of logical sense to me. I was deluding myself, because I couldn't live with the truth: that I would never feel Nola was safe again without my constant supervision.

When I snapped out of it, a song I hadn't heard since Marnie and I were in grade school had come on, and I realized Nola had grown silent. I rolled over onto my stomach to see she sat frozen, her face, framed under the little brown bangs Marnie cut with scissors on a kitchen stool, twisted into a rictus of fear.

"Nola," I said. She didn't respond, didn't take her eyes off the CD player we'd gotten for her fourth birthday, the little pink one with *Dora the Explorer* stickers plastered all over it. I snapped my fingers in front of her face and she didn't flinch. A runner of drool spilled from her lip and pattered on the carpet.

Was she having a seizure?

The chorus kicked in then, the choir singing of tiny hands in larger ones, of a love that could be seen as a crime. The words struck me like a hammer in the chest. Wanting to be her daddy. Her preacher. Suddenly the love song seemed sinister. When I reached to turn it off, an odd creeping sensation like when you're about to crush a particularly large and wriggly insect crawled up my spine.

The song stopped. Nola snapped out of her trance.

"Nola," I said. "Sweetheart, have you heard that song before?"

Nola shook her head violently, wide blue eyes obscured by her bangs as she looked down in curiosity at the drool spots on the floor. Though she'd never spoken a word about the monster who'd assaulted her, the trauma still far too pervasive, I felt certain he would have told her never to tell, that if she told on him he'd come to her house and murder her family or something equally abhorrent. I understood that fear, but rage overcame me, and I grabbed her arm, much rougher than I'd meant. "Nola, don't lie to Daddy."

I didn't realize Marnie had come home until I looked up in that awful moment to find her standing in the doorway. My hand fell away from Nola's tiny arm, the skin red in the shape of my fingers. Tears stood in Nola's eyes, though the look on her face was not pain but surprise. I'd never laid a finger on her for discipline until just then. Quite frankly, the look on my face in that moment probably mirrored hers.

There was no argument that night or ever. Marnie simply looked at me, straight into my heart where the poison had been festering. She took Nola by the hand, who'd run to her crying as the shock of what had happened finally struck her, and the two of them went upstairs to bed. I spent a few sleepless hours twisting back and forth on the couch under a small throw blanket. Eventually, I crept upstairs to my office and picked up the journal the family therapist had suggested I use to jot down what she'd called "irrational thoughts and/or behavior." I'd had neither the time nor inclination to use it, just left it on my desk to gather dust. What good would writing about it do? I needed *action*, not *words*.

When I opened it that night, I realized I'd been wrong about that. Marnie had been filling in the journal for me, and her words were exactly what I needed in that moment. Reading it made me sick, looking at my transformation through Marnie's eyes. In her words, it was like I'd been holding the family underwater, drowning us in my grief, determined to make Nola relive what that monster did to her over and over so she'd remember something, *anything*, about him: a smell, his voice, something about the place he took her, something about the rabbits. Dr. Ambrose might have held similar suspicions, but Marnie had known it in her bones I would never get past it, that I'd never wanted to. She'd known before I fully understood myself just how badly I'd wanted to hurt him, even *kill* him—to make the Rabbit Man suffer for what he'd done to our little girl. Our sweet Nola.

The next day I told Marnie my plan. All she did was sigh. As if it had been inevitable, like she'd been waiting for me to admit it. Finally she'd asked me, "Do you really think it's going to help her? Nola needs a father, not a vigilante." She'd told me if I went through with it to never come back.

That was just about a third of a year ago. This rain-soaked morning was the first time I'd been home since.

———

I FOUND THE little pink CD player right where I'd hidden it that night, under the musty old sleeping bag we'd used at the Grand Canyon the summer before Nola was born. I took that, too, and returned to Bookville shortly after one, dog-tired but eager to share my "find" with the others. The battery had died in Walker's RV a few weeks back, and our little area of the camp hadn't had music since. I was sure they would be pleased.

As I trudged down the concrete shoulder toward camp, I was reminded of a phrase from one of Nola's favorite picture books: *Under the bridge, where the Monsters live...* A story about a family of nice, cuddly monsters. *Here is that fabled place*, I thought. Only the monsters down here were most definitely not nice, and trying to cuddle one would be dangerous, like kissing a piranha.

"Look what I found," I said, holding up Nola's CD player.

The three of them looked up from their game of Rummy on a table made of plywood and wooden cable spools. Gonzalez's eyes lit up like a kid who'd just found the bra of his best friend's mom on their shower rod (though I suppose that wouldn't have interested him much even as a child). I plastered on a smile to cover for the sneer I felt trying to creep its way onto my face, having placed all bets on him.

He was my Rabbit Man. I was sure of it.

"Got batteries?" Walker asked.

"These ones still work," I said, and put it on the table by the discards.

"What's all this pink shit?" Popcorn wondered, eyeing me with suspicion. "You break your parole, or what?"

I pretended to be shocked. "Nah," I answered Popcorn. "Just found it. It's amazing what people will throw out on the street these days."

I popped the top open, revealing the mixed CD. The words FOR MARNIE had long faded, printed in block letters eleven or twelve years ago, the same words that had made Nola's eyes light up the night before I left her and her mother to live under the bridge with these animals.

"Still got a disc," Walker said. "Wonder who the fuck Marnie is?"

Again, I held back an unconscious sneer.

"That's the kind of question could get your ass in a whole lot of trouble," Popcorn said, before turning to me. "A'ight. Play that fuckin' music, white boy."

I sat down beside Gonzalez, who continued to eyeball the CD player the way Nola had that night in the living room, albeit somehow managing not to drool. One of the benefits of camping out close to the Bay, we could rinse our clothes out regularly or use laundry soap when we could find some. Hell, we could even give ourselves a good wash once in a while. Gonzalez wasn't most of us. He reeked of cigarettes and an omnipresent aroma of unwashed asshole. He hadn't brushed his teeth in months, maybe years. Sitting next to him you could imagine stink lines rising from his body, like that kid from *Peanuts*. It was difficult to sit so close to him, but I wanted him close when it happened.

This mound of dirt and repurposed trash under the Julia Tuttle Causeway was our living room. Graffiti on the pillars was the art on our walls. I pushed PLAY.

"Sympathy for the Devil" came on, over the shouts and laughter and music from the other encampments. Popcorn bit his lower lip and began to bob his head to the music.

Walker—who fucked girls, boys, adult women and once, according to his own account, a sedated gator—grew a sick smile. "I used to fuck to this song," he said, and stood up from the broken sofa to demonstrate, gyrating his hips with one hand at his side and the other holding down his imagined victim, be it human or animal.

"Sit your ass down," Popcorn said.

"You want some of this?" Walker said, thrusting his crotch toward the larger man.

"You best be gettin' your skinny dick outta my face." Popcorn picked up the discard pile from their Rummy game and threw the cards at Walker, who giggled and flopped back down on the couch.

"Man, you're pickin' those up!"

"Bull*shit.*"

Popcorn and Walker left the cards scattered on the ground and the ratty old sofa. I let the song play out, then skipped the next two. Still couldn't remember them, even if I tried.

"Hey, I like that song," Walker groaned about the second, but the next song had already started, the haunting chords on a keyboard, the *tss-tss-tss* of a hi-hat.

When George Michael began to sing in his raspy whisper, Gonzalez turned to me. He met my eyes for only a moment, but the shock was palpable, the guilt evident. He returned his gaze to the CD player, and as the song played out my eyes never left him. I felt them tearing up, thinking about what he must have done to my Nola, but I blinked it away. I couldn't let my grief, my anger, and a sudden disturbing rush of exhilaration from being so close after searching for so long come between me and my revenge. I studied Gonzalez with glistening eyes: this bland monster, this mild-mannered beast. I watched him and pictured my knife slipping into the hot meat between his ribs.

"*The fuck is that shit?*" someone called over, tearing me from my fantasy. I allowed my gaze to move beyond Gonzalez to the black '80s Chevy Impala resting beside a spray-painted entreaty that had once made the papers: *WE ARE NOT MONSTERS.* A guy I'd seen around a few times sat hanging out the driver door. He had a little mustache and silky blond hair like a man on a box of hair dye, except the circles under his eyes were so dark they could have been bruises.

"It's called music," Popcorn shouted back. "The fuck you think it is?"

The blond dude got out of his car and approached, snapping bubblegum. "Why you listenin' to that faggot, huh?"

"Actually, he's bisexual," Walker answered. "Not that it makes any goddamn difference."

"You listen to that shit, you're no better'n a faggot yourself." Blondie came right up to the table and reached for the CD player.

Popcorn swatted his hand away.

"Don't you fuckin touch me, nigger."

Popcorn's eyes narrowed. He grabbed the blond guy's arm and jerked it up behind his back, the kind of move a cop or someone who'd been trained in military might use, and I found myself suddenly glad to be up against Gonzalez instead of Popcorn.

"That's uncalled for," a woman I knew only as Pip shouted over to us.

Others crowded around. A man with a lisp and cargo shorts cinched high on his waist by a frayed piece of rope asked why we couldn't all just get along.

In the fracas, the blond dude stomped down on Popcorn's foot, chewing his gum with a gleeful. The heels of his cowboy boots sounded hard, and Popcorn's sneakers had seen better days. They were bound together by duct tape and falling apart at the seams, his tube socks so dirty they were black in places visible at the sides. Popcorn's howl of pain just about matched Mick Jagger's, and he let go of the blond dude's arm.

Blondie shook his hair as if Popcorn had just ruffled it instead of nearly breaking his arm, and then locked eyes with Gonzalez. The wretched little smelly man looked behind himself, shrinking from the cold gaze. Blondie had found his prey, a victim to reclaim his dominance. Before Gonzalez could scramble over the back of the couch, Blondie had yanked him back by his filthy jeans and began raining down on his back with balled-up fists, calling him *queer* and *runt* and *pussy*.

Whatever he was, Gonzalez was *mine*.

A surge of frenetic energy ran through me as I grabbed a fistful of Blondie's hair and yanked him away from Gonzalez, who used the distraction to squirm away. I threw a punch before Blondie could swing at me, clipping him in the jaw. Having never been in a fight before, only ever using my fists against inanimate objects, it stunned me how much of a rush I got from the feel of his jaw against my knuckles. The feeling was short-lived as Blondie slugged me hard in the gut. I staggered back, the breath knocked out of me, while Popcorn and Walker jumped in to pull Blondie back from doing me some real damage.

In all the commotion, Gonzalez had gotten up and was slinking off. I gathered up my strength and followed him. The ruckus of the other three men struggling and the crowd either egging them on or jeering them grew quieter the further Gonzalez and I ran.

This is it, I thought, feeling stronger and almost hyper-aware the closer I got to my quarry. I didn't think about going back home. I didn't think about Nola. All I could think of was *blood* and *blood* and *blood*...

———

I SUPPOSE I should tell you about the rabbits.

The day Nola ran away, Marnie and I had been fighting. Silly argument. She'd caught me smoking, something I hadn't done since she was pregnant—as far as she knew—and we'd gotten into it. She accused me of not caring to live long enough to see Nola graduate from college, and I accused her of not letting me relieve my stress the way I wanted. Nola heard us. She'd packed up some things in her knapsack: her stuffed lion Julio, which she spelled with a W-H-O, her favorite book about the elephant king, a bag of marshmallows (*mushmellows*, she called them), and a flashlight. I suspect she was going to camp out and roast her mushmellows over a fire, but how she'd planned to light one, I don't know. I suppose the thought might never have crossed a six-year-old's mind.

Whatever she'd gotten in her head, Nola sneaked out the back door while Marnie and I argued in raised whispers, knowing full well she could hear us despite the closed bedroom door. Somewhere after the corner of Day and Matilda, where a crossing guard told police she'd scolded Nola about crossing the street without looking both ways, our little girl disappeared.

Marnie noticed she'd slipped away just when we'd gotten to the root of the argument. At first, we thought she'd been playing. Nola had always loved hide and seek. So we looked in all the usual spots we might find her: behind the curtains, crouched behind the big ficus in my office, in the basement shower, or in her closet, under a pile of stuffed animals.

Nowhere. Anxiety grew to full-blown fear. She knew enough not to run away, but if she'd heard us arguing...

We searched outside, in the front and back yards, Marnie running out into the street and calling out her name. We phoned her friends, spoke to baffled, concerned parents. Finally, we called the police. Fifteen minutes later, officers showed up at our door. Marnie kept tugging at her shirt sleeves, pacing the room while the two officers took down what we had to tell them: what she was wearing, how old, hair color, about how tall, could she have gone to a relative's? I'd been watching Marnie unravel the whole time until she finally exploded, screaming at the officers, "Somebody's taken my baby and you're wasting our *fucking time!*" They'd looked at each other, offered their apologies, and then put out an AMBER alert.

While Marnie waited at the house for Nola to return, the both of us sick with the absolute certainty that at any moment they would call back to tell us they'd found her body in a ditch somewhere, I drove up and down the neighborhood. I scoured the grounds at Liz Virrick Park, where we often took her when neither of us were busy on the weekend. I even went to Nola's school, where Marnie taught the fourth grade, and I taught drama part-time to finance a failing career in screenwriting. Being there filled me with the dreadful certainty Nola would never have her mother as a teacher because some monster had taken her life.

Lost. Gone. Dead. My little girl is dead. These thoughts circled my mind as I drove through the neighborhood, once, twice, three times, certain I'd missed somewhere, hoping to return home to find her eating peanut butter out of the jar with her fingers, laughing at cartoons with her mother. But each time I returned, Marnie had been pacing the porch, or sitting, tugging at her shirt sleeves, and the house had been empty. I feared—*we* feared—there would never be laughter in that house again. So, back into the car, driving down the same streets, shouting her name as the neighborhood darkened.

It was just after 8 p.m. when the police called. My sweaty hand shook so badly the phone slipped into my lap. I pulled the car over and listened to the officer speak, holding the cell in a trembling hand as my heart pounded in my throat.

Imagination can be a terrible curse. I never saw it with my own eyes, but the image still haunts every waking moment of my life. It drove me to live among the sex offenders. It compelled me to find the monster who did it, the Rabbit Man, and to put him six feet in the fucking ground.

The sick fuck had left Nola naked beside a trash bin on the bare asphalt in an alley in Little Haiti. Eventually a busboy from a nearby restaurant had come out to dump his mop bucket and saw her shivering there. He'd called the police without going to her—worried, perhaps, that even attempting to help a naked child might be misconstrued as sexual abuse.

When Officer Sam Higgins arrived, he found a feral child huddled with her arms around her bruised knees, matted hair tangled in her face. Bleeding not just from the places she'd been violated, but from dozens of raised marks forensics later determined to be tiny scratches. Higgins wrapped the emergency blanket from his trunk around Nola, told her everything was going to be okay, that he was going to bring her to her mom and dad. At these words she leapt into his arms, latching around his neck, smearing his uniform with her blood.

The police were taking photographs of her injuries when I burst through the door, demanding to see her. Officer Higgins got in the way. Three officers had to hold me back from punching him, and if not for Sam's interference, I might have been charged with assaulting an officer. Sam and I hashed it out later. With two daughters himself, he keenly understood my rage. The Special Victims Bureau had taken over the case, but he'd promised to update me personally.

Marnie, Nola, and I went to the family therapist together. Dr. Ambrose had us explore our emotions in excruciating detail. She wanted us to open up, to work through our feelings, but each Thursday at 2 p.m. I begrudgingly entered her office and sat on that plush sofa entirely numb while Marnie droned and Nola played with toys in the corner. I saw no point to those visits; we were picking at scabs. While their meaningless words filled the terrifying silence, I sat alongside my wife, brewing hatred. My most violent fantasies were born in that room: gruesome acts I suspected I'd never be able to stomach even if the opportunity arose—thoughts which belonged to the monster growing inside me.

Eventually Dr. Ambrose accused me of stalling progress. I questioned her methods, her motives, called her a sadist. She asked me to leave. I apologized and she'd allowed me to return to the room. I'd lose myself in fantasy again. Several sessions passed this way, until our time was up.

Detective Rosario called a few weeks into this routine to inform us the lab had analyzed the white hairs they'd found on Nola's skin. Turned out to be animal fur, not human hair. They suspected the rapist kept rabbits, which kicked off a wide search for rabbit hutches in backyards and on rooftops.

Rosario didn't seem hopeful. By then, most registered sex offenders were living under the Tuttle Causeway, many of them already wearing ankle monitors.

I found myself driving several miles out of my way after work, slowing down over the water, catching a look at their tents and vehicles before driving ponderously back home. I'd seen them gathered down there, huddled from the rain, sharing food they'd scrounged, arguing, laughing. It all seemed normal and yet so alien to me. I wondered how they lived.

I wondered how they'd *bleed*.

Since I couldn't deal with the injuries to Nola's privates, I'd saddled Marnie with the unenviable task of applying ointment for several weeks before they healed. We spoke to each other less and less. We ate in front of the TV. I spent hours each night in the garage, pretending to work on the car. Mostly I would read my dad's old hunting magazines, fantasizing.

Late one night, Marnie entered the garage where I'd been sitting on a stool reading an old magazine, not even bothering to cover for the work I wasn't doing, and handed me the portable phone with no discernable expression in her gaze. I took it, listened to Sam Higgins apologize while feeling the floor drop out from beneath me, and mechanically thanked him for his help. Special Victims had made no progress in their search, and Nola had been unable to remember any details despite my coaching and our increasingly acrimonious sessions with Dr. Ambrose. Barring anything new, the case had effectively fizzled out. Went cold, like the darkened corners of my heart. After that, we never heard from him again. The Rabbit Man had gotten away.

That night I aimed to make sure it never happened again.

BREATHING HEAVILY, I caught up to Gonzalez near the fence at the base of the bridge and jerked him around roughly to face me.

"Hey! What gives?"

My vision was on a dimmer, timed to the unsteady beat of my heart. After that sucker punch from the blond dude and chasing after Gonzalez, I was on the verge of blacking out. But I would make sure he looked me in the eyes as the life drained out of him. I would make sure he knew what he'd done.

"*Nola*," I said. I shook him by his lumberjack jacket, raising a cloud of dust. "Nola, Nola," I blubbered, "my fucking *daughter*, you sick *fuck!*"

Mortified, Gonzalez threw his filthy hands in the air, a gesture of innocence. "Hey, no wait, man, I haven't—*done that*—for ten years! I slipped up *once*. I would never—I've *never*—I..."

I saw it dawn on him: first disgust, then fear, shock... and then confusion, suspicion. He looked over my shoulder, where the altercation had died down and Blondie was walking backwards to his car, shouting curses and kicking the dirt. "You have a *daughter*?"

My grip on him lessened. I grabbed him harder, attempting to embolden myself. "Bullshit!"

"I swear, I haven't—" Gonzalez couldn't say the words, as if his own crime disgusted him. "Not since, you know, back then. I served my time. She's *forgiven* me. I swear to Jesus, man, I haven't done it again since!"

I felt the monster inside me step back from its cage. Gradually, I let Gonzalez go. He brushed his jacket off as if I was the one who'd made him dirty. "I'm sorry," I said as a cloud of dust rose around us.

"It's okay. I'm fine." With another look over my shoulder his eyes narrowed, and he returned his gaze to me. "You know, I knew there was something not right about you when you first came down here. Something about the way you moved. Not quite Walker's swagger, more like you were looking down your nose at us." He shook his head. "And that story about your niece? The things you said you did to her..."

Gonzalez trailed off, swallowing hard, avoiding the unpleasant terminology.

I'd noticed him wincing as we listened to Walker describe his escapades in nasty detail. All this time I thought Gonzalez had just been putting on a show, the way some of the most vile politicians and religious figures act sanctimonious when inside they were repugnant.

"I didn't buy that for a second," he finished.

"You didn't?"

Gonzalez shook his head.

"Why not?"

"It's like there was nothing there," Gonzalez said, and gestured toward his own face. "In your eyes. No regret. No pride. No *lusting*, like the way how Walker talks about his..." Another hard swallow. "Just this blank look. A *dead* look."

I regarded him silently.

"So you think somebody here—what? They—*did something*—to your little girl?"

I nodded, feeling like a fool. All this time it had been so plain to Gonzalez I was a fraud, it must have been obvious to the others. Fear crept into my nerves, setting the monster back on edge. I would have to be more careful.

"Why did you think it was me?"

It took a moment for me to realize what he was asking. "The song," I told him. "The way you reacted to it, I just figured..." I didn't need to mention the rabbit. It didn't seem smart to reveal such evidence.

"Which song? That '80s one?"

I'd nearly blown it all because of that song. Again, I nodded.

"It wasn't the song," Gonzalez said. "It's the tape player. It's the exact same..." He shook his head, his eyes downcast, and with that look I understood. His own victim must have had the same CD player. He hadn't been reacting to the song at all. "Anyway," he said, "I wasn't the one acting strange. Popcorn and Telly, those guys started a fight over it."

"Telly? He the blond guy?"

Gonzalez was about to speak when the blip of a siren startled us both. We turned to look as a police cruiser crawled into the center of camp, parting the crowd. Miami P.D. swinging by for a routine check, although just as often they came through to harass the residents. Some of these men and women had parole terms stating no alcohol or illicit drugs. Others weren't allowed to be within a certain distance of other offenders, which didn't make much sense under the bridge, where everyone was here for the same basic reason. Most of the cops who came through here were just looking for a reason to use unacceptable force. For the most part, I wouldn't say I could blame them.

Gonzalez shifted nervously in the dirt. The cop got out of the car and headed over to a huddled group of sex offenders. As he turned in the direction of the scuffle, fear struck me and I hid my face, muttering, "Shit!"

Officer Sam Higgins' bald head gleamed as he patted a woman in boxer shorts and galoshes on the shoulder and passed a bottle of water to an elderly man I didn't recognize. New people wandered in here every day, as more and more were forced to sign the registry, many for petty offences. Higgins checked on a guy's ankle monitor. The guy—Dolph, I think—offered his hand, and Higgins shook it without hesitation.

It amazed me to see how humanely he treated these people, knowing some of them could easily have victimized his own children. It was clear he believed in basic human decency, though if he'd caught these same people in a crime I was certain he wouldn't hesitate to tackle the prick and put him in the back of his cruiser, maybe put a little more elbow into the bust than was necessary. He was a cop after all, not Gandhi. But the fact that a man who dealt with the absolute worst of humanity every single day could still find a moment to be charitable gave me a glimmer of hope.

As I watched him smile and shake hands, I felt like I could forget about the Rabbit Man. I could leave here and never come back. I could return to my long-suffering wife, to my courageous little girl who had somehow managed to put her assault in the past while her father continued to grieve.

Sam laughed at something one of the men said and got back in his cruiser. I watched him drive back to the topside of the Tuttle, watched everyone return to whatever they'd been doing. I felt myself relax.

"You know, if it's anyone here, I'd put money on Telly," Gonzalez said, dragging me right back down.

"Why him?" I snapped.

"I just overheard him bragging once, about all the stuff he'd gotten away with. He said he—"

It was clear he couldn't repeat the actual words Telly had used. "You don't have to say it."

Gonzalez gave a brief smile. "Thanks. He did it to a little girl, and all they got him on was grooming some cop on the 'net posing as an eight-year-old."

Down there among the others, the blond guy, Telly, chucked a stone in the direction the cop car had gone, having since recaptured his bravado. I watched him swagger back to his own car, chewing his gum with his mouth open. He climbed in and slammed the squeaky door behind himself.

"You're gonna kill him, aren't you?"

I thought about the scratches, the rabbits. My mind ran through all the gruesome scenarios I'd dreamed up during our sessions with Dr. Ambrose. "What if I said yes?"

Gonzalez followed my gaze. Telly had his dirty work boots rested on the driver's window. Behind the windshield, the orange ember of his cigarette burned.

"I won't tell," Gonzalez said. "He'll just do it again, the second he gets a chance. You can tell just by looking at him. Heck, I wouldn't be surprised if that's what he does at night, driving off all by himself."

I considered this in silence, knowing the decision had already been made for me.

———

EXCEPT FOR THOSE times he left camp well after sundown, I didn't let Telly leave my sight again for over a week. He'd recline the driver's seat and nod off as the sun began to sink beyond the skyline, well before anyone else had even considered sleep. Later, when most of us had been out for a few hours, I'd watch him light up a smoke in the dark behind the windshield. Then he'd creep out with the running lights off. A few hours later, he'd pull back into his spot. I'd watch him fire up a butt with his Zippo, lighting a dark smile on his face. The little orange ember of his cigarette would wax and wane. After a few minutes, he'd flick it out the window in a shower of sparks, put his booted feet out the window, and go back to sleep. Once, he'd gone directly to the water and washed his hands. To wash off what, I don't know.

But I can guess.

About a week into this routine, Telly left the car to go

down to the water to fish. (We caught a fair few down in that part of Biscayne Bay. Going hungry was never a worry for us living under the bridge, though I lost the taste for fish quickly.) I wandered over to the car, curiosity getting the best of me, and peeked in the dusty window. The passenger seat was covered in cassette tapes, mostly metal and hard rock bands: AC/DC, Iron Maiden, Metallica, Slayer. With a collection like that, it wasn't likely he'd have ever listened to George Michael, but I considered it might be a part of his pathology, like maybe he'd been abused to it when he was younger. Or maybe it reminded him of a junior school crush. Parking tickets were scattered on the floor like the bottom of a birdcage.

I spotted what I'd been hoping to find hanging from the rearview mirror. Due to the fine layer of dust on the windshield, I hadn't been able to see it before. A little white rabbit's foot swayed gently on a bathtub chain, a few spots of something dark on its fur. I shaded my eyes against the glass for a closer look, thinking it might just be blood.

"Lookin' for somethin', asshole?"

I stepped away, caught. Telly sauntered back with the fishing pole over his shoulder and no fish. I stammered something about looking for cigarettes, and Telly narrowed his eyes.

"You want a smoke, you coulda just ast." Chewing absently on a wad of pink gum, he reached into the back pocket of his jeans and pulled out a pack of Camels, shifting the pole to his other shoulder. He shook one out and flicked it at me.

I caught it, fumbled it into the dirt. I picked it up and blew on it, then nestled it between my lips. The sweet smell of tobacco filled my nostrils. Marnie and I had quit when we found out she was pregnant. I'd sneaked a few puffs here and there after Nola was born, but after Marnie caught me lighting up the day of the argument, the day Nola ran away, I hadn't smoked since.

"Got a light?"

He threw a Zippo at me, and I caught it deftly. Lit the smoke. Inhaled. The first drag felt like pins jabbing my lungs. After that, the drags were smoother. "Thanks," I said, holding the cigarette between my teeth as I handed the Rabbit Man his lighter.

"No problem." A buzz had him reaching into the back pocket of his jeans. He opened the flip phone and studied the message. "Gotta split," he said. He opened the car door, then squinted at me. "Hey, no hard feelings about that love tap last week. I woulda hit me, too, if they'da been my buddies you was messin' with."

"They're not my buddies. Thanks again for the smoke," I added, walking away.

"Any time, amigo. Just stay the fuck away from my car next time."

I lied and said I would.

IT WAS TWO nights later when I dared approach his car again. He was asleep inside, his boots on the dash. I crept up to the driver door and listened to his slow, deep breathing for a while, maybe too long. I needed to be sure he was sleeping. I wanted to catch him off guard. He looked at peace. Like he'd slept well. It enraged me to see that, when my own sleep was so fitful because of him.

I wondered how many other children he might have

abused since the police sent him down here, how many child-hoods he'd taken away. How many families he'd destroyed. How many fathers he'd poisoned, the way he poisoned me. I still knew nothing about him, but none of that mattered. I could have called in with Officer Higgins' badge number, got them to run Telly's plates. I could have found a previous address. I could have rented a car—unless Marnie had cancelled my credit cards, which was possible—and followed him the next time he left camp. I didn't do any of these things. I didn't want to know about his life. All I wanted was for it to be him, and for it to end *tonight*.

I rounded the dirty front of the car to the passenger side. Ever so gently, I pulled up the handle. The door came open an inch with a click that seemed to rebound off the cement pillars and the underside of the bridge. Telly snored and shifted in his sleep. I froze, blood hammering. We were mere feet from each other, but his car was far enough away from the rest of Bookville, a pariah among pariahs, that I thought I'd be safe from potential witnesses. Despite the distance, if he woke up and saw me looming over him, no doubt he'd shout, and my whole stupid reckless plan, the months of research and preparation and time away from the girls, all of it would have been for nothing.

I held my breath.

He didn't wake.

Slowly, I pulled the door open. The amount of times I'd watched him open it to get one thing or another, I knew it wouldn't creak, not like the driver door. I knew the dome light wouldn't come on, either; it had burned out or didn't work. I slipped in cautiously beside him and pulled the door closed.

Telly slept with his seat reclined, his knees curled up to

his chest. He breathed deeply, a sure sign he was either asleep or faking it, ready to gut me like he gutted fish with the jagged hunting knife attached to his belt.

His eyes suddenly snapped open and he scrambled up against the door, sucking in a breath with childlike terror before squinting at me coolly. His breath smelled like cinnamon when he said, "What the fuck do you want?"

"Roll up your window."

"Why the fuck should I?" He looked in the direction I indicated: the tip of my father's old buck knife aimed at the faded crotch of his tight jeans. "*Jesus*, man," he said on exhale and rolled up the window, not taking his eyes off me. "You mind tellin' me what the fuck you're doin' in my car? And don't say you're lookin' for a cigarette, amigo, 'cause I know you ain't a smoker."

For a long while, I said nothing. All the time I'd spent dreaming about this moment, it felt like he should know why I was here before I took his life away. It felt like I should make him aware, for Nola's sake if not mine. But everything I started to say seemed wrong. Like I'd be offering him an explanation he surely didn't deserve. Like I'd be allowing him the opportunity for forgiveness when forgiveness had never been an option.

"Take out the tape," I said finally.

"What?"

"*The tape. Take out the fucking tape.*"

"All right, man. *Shit.*" Eyeing me the whole time, Telly reached for the cassette player in the dash. His dirty fingers found the eject button and he pushed it. The tape popped out with a satisfying clunk. Telly fumbled it into his hand, then held it up for me to see. "All right?"

"All right," I said, and thrust the knife at his crotch.

Telly's eyes opened wider than I'd thought humanly possible, like something you'd see on a Saturday morning cartoon. He made to cry out, but I pressed a hand over his mouth, his mustache prickling against my palm, his tongue flicking out, probably involuntarily, as I mashed his head against the doorjamb.

Relishing the agonized terror in his eyes, I missed the sight of his hand scrabbling for the knife at his hip. He had it pulled out and pain tore up my chest before I could react. Smashing his head back against the door, I thrust my elbow against his wrist, pushing it back. I shoved my knee down hard against his legs, yanking on the knife in his groin. It came free with a jet of blood that splashed my wrist, his jeans already dark with it.

The wet blade gleamed in the arc lights as I pulled it back to strike again, and I shoved it straight into his throat, to the hilt. The monster's tongue flicked against my palm as his life spurted out from the hole in his neck, soaking my shirt. His legs kicked weakly, like a dying insect's. A gout of blood poured from the hole as he gagged. His fingers relaxed, dropping his knife. The life left his eyes.

I sat there a moment longer, watching his body leak blood, listening for his breath. I couldn't believe he was dead, that it was finally over and I could leave this godforsaken place and return to my family.

His cell phone buzzed.

I wondered who would be texting so late. I couldn't imagine it being a booty call, although I supposed like Walker he could have had a thing for women and men as well as children.

I told myself it was over. But the cell phone buzzed

again, and I couldn't resist opening the glovebox, from which I'd located the sound on the second buzz.

Two items fell from the glovebox on a landslide of junk paper and Big Red chewing gum wrappers: Telly's crappy flip phone, and a heavy black revolver.

I picked up the phone, giving the gun a wary look, as if it was a dangerous animal.

Two new messages awaited, both from Unknown Number.

The second message was an address. I knew the area. Somewhere in Coconut Grove, where the rich folk live.

The first message said: ARE U IN?

Was I in? Hell, I didn't even know what I was in *for*—but I'd already come this far.

What if Telly had an accomplice? I thought. Someone with the resources to keep him from falling under the scrutiny of the Miami-Dade P.D. Someone rich enough to live in Coconut Grove.

I had to find out.

I scrolled through prior messages phone, looking at his responses. They were curt replies, mostly written in text-speak. No wonder, with the ancient buttons on the thing. Heart hammering, I thumbed the buttons, clicking ponderously through numbers and letters to type out: B THERE IN 1 HR

I wasn't sure how soon they'd be expecting him, but I wanted to give myself enough time to get cleaned up first.

The phone buzzed again in my hand.

MAKE IT TWO, BACK DOOR'S OPEN

Even better, I thought.

Telly's body slid another few inches toward the floor. In the dim light beyond the space he'd left, I spotted Gonzalez huddled against a pillar, watching us with wide eyes. I wondered how long he'd been standing there. Long enough, I guessed.

His eyes met mine, and he nodded. Somehow, I managed to nod back.

I dragged Telly's lifeless body out of the seat and climbed over him, then sat him up in the passenger seat. Reaching over him, I half-expected him to snap awake and grab me around the throat. Of course he didn't. And when I yanked on the seat adjuster, he dropped back along with the seat.

I flicked the dome light to its off position, and started the engine. The Impala purred like a panther. The running lights already off, I backed up, and drove out up the embankment, leaving behind Bookville for good.

As I drove west on I95, the rabbit's foot jingled on its chain from the mirror. In all the commotion, I'd forgotten about it. I tore it down to get a better look. The dark stains were no doubt blood. Whether it was old blood or new I couldn't tell, not when I'd just smeared Telly's blood onto its dirty off-white fur.

I tucked the totem into my pocket and looked at myself in the rearview. A few streaks of blood had spattered my face, and I wiped them off with the back of my hand. I didn't plan to go home looking like I did, anyway.

At my old 24-hour gym, I parked the car at the far corner of the lot, under a broken streetlamp. There was a blanket in the backseat, which I threw over Telly's body. When I got out, it felt like I'd given my whole body a workout, every muscle aching.

I staggered to the brightly lit gym. The doors slid open for me.

The attendant, a young kid with clear, tanned skin,

gave me a funny look. When I got into the showers, I understood why. I hadn't been into the city for a week, hadn't shaved, hadn't slept. My shirt was gouged open at the chest, matted to my skin with blood. I looked like a man who'd gotten lost in the jungle, fought a wild animal, and narrowly escaped with his life. I left the showers clean and shaven, my wound—Telly's blade had cut my left nipple in half—washed and dressed with paper towels, surprised that the kid wiping down the equipment hadn't called the cops. Far enough away from the mess I'd left under the Tuttle, I had no worries they would finger me for the crime even if the kid called in my appearance and had them pull the security video. For all they knew, I'd taken time off work to deal with the aftermath of what had happened to Nola.

Back at the Impala, I rooted through a duffel bag of clean-smelling clothes in the trunk. Telly was about my size, and always seemed to be dressed in a t-shirt and a fresh pair of jeans. I assumed on some of his excursions he'd been to use a laundromat, but I suppose his friend in the Grove could have easily gotten them washed for him.

I found black jeans a t-shirt and as worn Miami Heat cap, and put them on in the dark below the burnt-out street-lamp. The jeans were snug and a little short, but the t-shirt fit well enough. Though they were clean, they felt slimy on my skin and scalp. To be wearing the clothes of the man who'd assaulted my little girl... but it was a necessary evil.

Walk a mile in a man's shoes, I thought. When I got back in the car, I gave Telly's pale, dead face a long hard look.

This was somebody's son. Someone had given birth to this monster. Had *raised* it.

Not wanting to give him another moment of my time, I

started the car, and headed toward the Grove. He was fertilizer now. Worm food.

The streets out here were bright even in the dead of night. Palms in front of multimillion-dollar homes swayed in a breeze from the bay. I read house numbers on pillars and porticos and wrought iron arches until finally I found the house.

I parked the Impala on the next block, left it there, and headed back on foot.

The whole neighborhood felt eerily quiet, aside from the gentle swish of the tide, and the palm fronds above. I imagined the people who lived here, in their Xanax-induced slumbers, some maybe burning the midnight oil to keep the creditors at bay. Was it possible a predator lived among them? I was certain there were tax-evaders. Philanderers. Pill addicts. Spouse abusers. Investment swindlers. Perpetrators of criminal negligence—even potential vehicular homicides.

I wondered how many sex offenders had once lived on my own street.

The house stood silent before me, the moon casting a diamond glint trail on the bay beyond. A security camera watched over the gate, the stone wall around the perimeter lined with bushes. Spotlights lit the glass house's exterior, but inside the only room that appeared lit was the kitchen.

As I headed along a red clay path toward the beach in the darkness below the wall, the sound of the ocean grew louder. My feet more sore than they'd been the day I'd walked home, I longed to take off my shoes and walk in the sand. But more pressing business was at hand.

The gun felt heavy against my spine, tucked into the back of Telly's jeans.

On the beach, I crept close to the wall, looking for a point of egress, certain the owner had access to the docks dotting a strip of white sand. Finally, I reached a small gate where the wall dipped down on either side. No camera in sight. The gate locked, I climbed over the wall and jumped down on the other side, praying they didn't have dogs.

The water beat against the shore, almost as loud as my heart thrumming in my ears.

The house, a series of stacked white stucco-and-glass rectangles, stood quiet and stark against the moonlit sky. I could see a camera above the back door, and I slowed my approach, pulling the peak of the Heat cap down to hide my face. I rounded the pool, spotting children's pool toys floating in the blue-green water, lit from below. Stepped over a damp towel left bunched on the concrete, and a small pair of sopping wet board shorts with little flamingos printed on them left halfway to the door, as if they'd been cast off on the way to the house.

I stood under the camera, and jiggled the handle. No luck.

Out of options, short of smashing one of the window walls and announcing the presence of an intruder, I thumbed the doorbell.

As I waited for a response, I felt sick creeping into my throat, and swallowed it down, hard.

"That you, Tell?"

A male voice over the intercom. Deep. He sounded drunk.

I nodded, not wanting to show my face but desperate to make the man believe I was Telly. Inspiration struck, and I dug into the jeans, thankful I'd thought to transfer it from my pants when I'd changed out of them.

I held up the rabbit's foot. Jingled it on the chain.

The door buzzed.

"C'mon downstairs," the man said. "The party's started."

I stepped inside.

The darkened house smelled of burning incense. Beer. Lit dimly by the moon over the bay, the living room looked as though someone had been having a party. From deeper inside the house, music thumped. Just the bass, but I recognized the song. I'd heard it in nightmares so often the beat was seared into my brain. I swallowed bile, and continued toward a brightened doorway.

Stairs led down. Basements were rare in Miami—hell, in most of South Florida. Near the beach, you'd have to drill through several feet of coral rock before you hit water. It was difficult to dig, and even more to keep them dry.

I drew the revolver from the back of Telly's jeans. I'd already checked to see that it was loaded. I wasn't sure what I would find down there, but with the boy's swim trunks at the pool, and whoever lived in this house being a friend of Telly's, I felt it best to err on the side of caution.

Creeping down, I held the gun pointed at the doorway, expecting someone to step out at the foot of the stairs with every step down, the song so loud it felt like the music penetrated every pore in my body. I realized halfway down the stairs that I'd been crying.

As I descended further, a room came into view below, oddly incongruous to the modern style of the house above, as if someone had torn it straight from a magazine from the '80s. Faux wood paneling. A brown tartan sofa with colorful afghan throw pillows. An ancient game system resting on the floor, hooked up to a large tube television with knobs instead of buttons above the brown speaker panel. The smell of beer was even stronger. Several empty bottles stood on the coffee table, some with the labels peeled off.

I reached the clean concrete floor, and turned.

The boy was stretched out naked on the red fabric of a pool table, his frail limbs spread wide, hands and feet pointing toward the corner holes. He looked about nine or ten, the conspicuous lack of pubic hair at his groin and under his armpits evidence of his young age. He appeared asleep, but was more likely passed out or drugged. If so, he was lucky not to be subjected to the sight of the two men watching him.

On either side of the boy, two deeply tanned men stood stripped down to the waist. One wore boxer shorts, the other tight blue briefs, his erect penis sprung from the y-front. The man in boxers, his hair slicked back like Gordon Gecko, stroked himself with one hand while leering down at the boy, taking a swig of beer with the other.

"Father Figure," blasting from a large wood cabinet stereo, ended.

The man in the briefs kneaded the foreskin-hooded end of his penis as if he were chalking a pool cue. In the silence, he groaned. Neither man had seen me—yet.

I snapped back the hammer.

The man in boxers turned to me, the bottle dropping from his hand as he realized I wasn't Telly.

"What the—?"

The pistol silenced him before the bottle hit even the floor, the bullet tearing into his shoulder and spinning him around on his bare feet with a spray of blood, DayGlo under the fluorescent track lights. He fell back against the pool table, his arm squeaking as he slid down to the floor on his butt in a puddle of beer and broken glass.

The song started up again, on repeat: *Tss-tss-tss...*

Briefs had reached into one of the pockets and grabbed a pool ball while I'd watched the Boxer Shorts fall. As he threw it at me, his hard-on bounced in an almost comical way, making me think of those Follow the Bouncing Ball singa-longs from old cartoons.

I ducked, but not before it struck me in the chest, just above the nipple Telly had slashed open. I fired again. The shot went wild, striking the wall a foot from his face, taking a chunk out of the wood wallpaper.

He tore a pool cue off the rack and gripped it in both hands, holding the felt-tipped end pointed at the boy's scrawny chest.

"Don't fucking shoot, man, I swear to God—"

This time, my aim was true.

I approached Boxer Shorts as he tried to pull himself to his feet, his blood-streaked hand constantly slipping on the wood of the pool table so he kept falling back on his ass in the spilled beer.

"Please, don't kill me, man," he wept. "I'm sick." He blub-bered, lips quivering, tears streaming down his face. "I'm just sick!"

"I know," I said, and shot him in the head.

THE WALK BACK to Telly's Impala was excruciating. I kept thinking somebody must have heard the shots. Someone must have called the police. But the cops never showed. The streets remained empty and silent, just the sound of the breaks hitting the sand accompanying me to where Telly's body awaited disposal.

I filled the small gas can from the tank with a syphon I

found in the trunk, and splashed the gas around the front and back seats, drenching Telly. I tossed the gun in through the passenger window, followed by the gas tank.

Telly's Zippo lit on the first strike. I stepped back, and threw it in.

The fire caught fast. I was already on my way back to the beach when the gas can exploded, and I turned back to see the Impala shoot into the air, flames spewing from shattered glass as it crashed back down on burst tires.

The boy was sitting where I'd left him. I'd carried him upstairs and dressed him in the living room, where they'd left his clothes. He didn't weigh much, maybe sixty pounds soaking wet. His eyes fluttered as I carried him down through the darkened residential streets. Police sirens blared by on the block opposite, heading toward the fire, but somehow we remained unseen.

I carried the boy as far as Mercy Hospital. With the cap peak still obscuring my face, I brought him into Emerg, which seemed eerily empty. As I laid him out on a gurney, a night nurse came down the hall with a clipboard. She called after me as I rushed off, ignoring her, glad the boy would be safe in her care.

As I walked home, I thought about what Marnie had said to me the day I left. Nola may not have needed a vigilante. She would certainly have preferred I'd never left, that I'd stayed home to be a father to her and watch over her. But I'm certain the boy, had he known how close he'd come to being violated and most likely murdered that night, might not feel the same.

It broke my heart to know things between Marnie and I would never be the same, no matter how hard I tried. Even if she'd have me back, our time apart would always be between us. The Rabbit Man's death, and those nameless men whose lives I'd taken in a basement in Coconut Grove, would seep into every seemingly pleasant conversation, every social engagement, every one of Nola's milestones. In the back of my mind and hers, the Rabbit Man would still be running.

Back at the house in Coral Gables, I used my key in the door, pleased for a second time to find it still worked. I crept up to our bedroom, saw Marnie sleeping with legs stretched over my side of the bed. It had been four months since we'd slept in that bed together, and she still slept mostly on her side.

I slipped by into Nola's room. The moon illuminated her head against the pillow. Nola had a thumb in her mouth, a habit she'd grown out of at age four but had taken up again in the wake of her experience with the Rabbit Man.

My sweet little girl's eyes opened wide as she drew the covers up to her chin, and for a terrible moment I flashed back to the eerily similar look Telly had given me when I woke him with the knife. Nola relaxed, seeing it was me.

"I thought you were a monster," she said.

I wondered, *Am I?*

Could I tell her there was nothing to be afraid of, that there were three less monsters in the world because of what I'd done that night? I flashed on the tape in Telly's hand, completely unreadable in the dark. It could have been a polka album for all I'd cared. That splotch on the rabbit's foot could have been dirt or paint or just about anything.

Could I tell her I'd taken pleasure in killing those two men?

There was no doubt in my mind what they'd intended to do with that boy. But what was Telly's role in it? Had he in fact been the Rabbit Man I'd so wanted him to be? I'd *needed* him to be, so I could come home to my wife? To our daughter?

Marnie had been right after all: Nola didn't need a vigilante. I'd needed to *be* one.

I'd fooled myself into believing that killing the Rabbit Man was about seeking justice for my little girl, but it had never been for her. I'd needed to take him out of the world to feel strong again. I needed to erase him from our family history to cover for my own shame, my own weakness. So I wouldn't feel like a coward anymore.

So *I* would feel safe.

It had never been about justice. And the fear, that *shame* —it would never end.

There were more of them, you see. I'd forgotten about Telly's cell phone tucked into the back pocket of his jeans. And as I crossed the South Dixie Highway on my way back home, it had buzzed against my pelvis.

TOMORROW NIGHT, the text said. U IN?

Was I in? No question.

But first I needed to buy a gun.

I smiled down at Nola, her face half in darkness, my shadow drawn long over her bed. "No, honey," I told her, faking a reassuring smile. "It's me. Daddy's home."

NOTES: A shorter version of this story was originally published in KnightWatch Press's *What Goes Around* anthology. When the rights were reverted to me I decided to release it as a standalone novella to be given away free to attract new readers (or, I suppose, repel them). Doing so gave me a chance to go through it again with fresh eyes. I'd never felt fully satisfied with the story, and the reason for that was Telly the pedophile, otherwise known as "the Rabbit Man"—or is he?—had ended up being the only *true* monster in the story and since he ended up being such a pathetic monster, it just didn't feel like enough.

Everything after Telly's death in the car to the final scene with the narrator's daughter was added to give the story a more rich scope. The texts, the possibility of an underground pedophile ring... and the idea that the narrator, despite his reservations that he might have become a Nietzschean monster, decides to continue what he'd started. None of this was in the original story.

The reason I included it here? People have been asking for a paperback version of this story for years, and I felt like now was the time to provide one.

IMAGINARY MONSTERS
A SCREENPLAY

<u>TEASER</u>

FADE IN:

EXT. WOODS - MORNING

Sneakers CRUNCH over dead leaves, running. Rubber boots follow close behind, tracking mud.

The sneakers belong to BREEN, 13 and having an awkward time with puberty. He laughs wildly. The boots are SARAH's, 14 and dressed in a hoodie and jeans, chasing Breen. Both kids carry fishing poles, tackle boxes RATTLING as they kick through the underbrush and weave between the evergreens.

                    SARAH
        I'm gonna get you, Breen O'Brien!

BREEN
In your dreams, butt-nut!

With an OUTRAGED ROAR, Sarah breaks into a full run.

Beams of sunlight fall through a canopy of leaves.

Breen kicks through low branches and young pines.

Giggling, breath sharp. With a backward glance he sees she's right behind him.

The trees thin out ahead, glints of sunlight on a lake beyond. Breen lets out a surprised laugh, darting forward with renewed vigor.

EXT. DEEP BOG LAKE - MORNING

Breen stumbles out of the woods, breathing heavy.

Sarah CRASHES out from him. Her breath catches in her chest at the sight of the beautiful lake, round and dark and peaceful. GULLS CRY as they rise from a thin mist on the surface. Beyond, mountains touch the sky.

SARAH
It's amazing!

Breen just smiles.

They head down to a ROWBOAT tied to a tree, half on shore.

Breen unties the boat and heaves it into the lake. Already hooking a worm, Sarah flinches as he jumps in.

                    BREEN
                (re: his hook)
                Do mine?

                    SARAH
                Wimp.

Breen winces as she hooks the worm on it.

The rowboat drifts in the middle of the lake. Sarah casts her line. So does Breen. Bobbers bob on the calm water.

    Reeling in his line, Breen throws a longing glance at Sarah. She catches him.

                SARAH (CONT'D)
            What? I got worm on my face?

He turns away, going red. She smiles, pleased with herself.

                SARAH (CONT'D)
        How'd you find out about this place, anyways?

                    BREEN
        My dad used to take me when I was little. He told
        me once about this fish he caught that was so big, it
                dragged him all around the lake.

                    SARAH
                Cool...

BREEN

Actually it was cold because he fell in the lake!

Breen winces again at his lame joke, hiding his embarrass-
ment by casting out his line. Sarah watches the worm
PLUNK into the water. The LINE JERKS immediately,
then WHIZZES off.

Breen grips the rod, tugging back.

The handle SPINS like a fan blade, catching his thumb. He
cries out and he lets go of the rod. The spool ZIPS as it
unravels.

Startled, Sarah bumps her pole. It SPLASHES into the
water, sinking to the dark bottom. She moans in disappointment before returning her attention to Breen.

In the darkness below, a GIGANTIC SLITTED EYE
blinks!

Breen's lure continues its beeline toward the mountains. The
line runs out. The reel sticks.

He holds on tight, planting his feet on the hull, causing the
boat to LURCH forward.

SARAH

Let it go!

BREEN

My dad gave me it!

Sarah grabs his hands and peels his fingers off the rod. It
SPLASHES into the water. The boat slows to a stop and
rocks gently as the kids breath a sigh of relief.

Sarah's shriek breaks the silence.

SARAH
Something just touched my arm!

Breen gives her a skeptical look. Then a BLACK
TENTACLE wriggles out of the water behind her and his
eyes widen. He reaches blindly, fingers searching. Finally,
they settle on an oar.

Sarah sees his fear and matches it. She turns to look.

BREEN
No, don't—!

Too late. She screams and dives for cover.

Breen raises the oar to swing—

—as the tentacle swoops down at Sarah! A SECOND
TENTACLE grabs the oar and wrenches it from Breen's
hand. He screams.

A tentacle grabs Sarah's leg. It's black with rows of
TOOTHY SUCKERS that tear into her shin. Watery blood
oozes out.

SARAH
BREEEEN!

Breen rushes for her, nearly tipping the boat. He grabs under her arms and pulls. Tears roll down their cheeks.

> BREEN
> I've got you, Sarah! I've got you!

> SARAH
> Don't let me go, please don't let me go!

For a moment it seems like she might get free. There's hope in their eyes. Then she's yanked from his arms and into the water.

Breen scuttles to the edge and peers in.

> BREEN
> Sarah! *Sarah!* SARAH!!!

His SCREAMS carry over the dark lake... through the trees... to a DIRT ROAD. Alongside it, a road sign quivers— WELCOME TO DARK PINES—and the sound of an APPROACHING CAR overtakes Breen's cries.

Finally, a HYBRID with a U-Haul trailer RUMBLES past.

INT./EXT. PAUL'S HYBRID - MORNING

The backseat's jam-packed with luggage and garbage bags. DR. PAUL DARLING drives, an unshaven late-30s, blazer-and-T-shirt kind of guy, enjoying the view as the car weaves through evergreens, past low mountains and sheer granite.

NOELLE DARLING, 16 and deep into a Hot Topic-goth phase, listens to MUSIC while texting on her phone, oblivious to the natural wonders.

NOELLE (TEXT)
Ugh nature! Get me outta here!!

TAYLOR (TEXT)
lol we miss you Noelle, come visit soon!

A DEER grazes near the ditch. It stares at Paul as they drive by. He's shaken by it, the closeness of nature.

Noelle looks up to find him peering at her quizzically. She takes out an earbud.

NOELLE
What?

PAUL
You just missed a deer.

NOELLE
(unenthused)
Oh. Neat.

She returns to her phone.

Paul shakes his head and rolls down his window. He takes a deep breath of fresh mountain air. Exhales happily.

As they drive further down the road, running parallel to a creek and beyond a mill and a farmer's field, the trees open on the PICTURE POSTCARD TOWN of Dark Pines.

EXT. DR. BASWELL'S HOUSE - DAY

A gorgeous old three-story gingerbread-style house, with a sign by the sidewalk:

> DR. T. BASWELL, Psy.D.
> Mon - Thurs, 8AM - 4PM
> Walk-Ins Appreciated!

The Hybrid parked in the driveway, Paul and Noelle unload baggage from the backseats onto the porch.

NOELLE
Dad? How come the sign doesn't say your name?

PAUL
Because it's Dr. Baswell's house.

NOELLE
So we're just supposed to live in someone else's house?

PAUL
Dr. Baswell was my professor in college. I made a promise a long time ago I'd take over his practice if anything ever happened to him.

> NOELLE
> So did he die, or...?

> PAUL
> Nobody knows. A couple of weeks ago, his patients
> showed up for their sessions and he didn't.

Noelle looks up at the house, the widow's watch, the dark windows like soulless eyes.

> NOELLE
> This place looks haunted.

Paul flashes a grin and tosses her a bag. She fumbles it.

> PAUL
> You don't believe in ghosts, do you, Noelle?

> NOELLE
> Dad. Of course not. I was kidding.

Paul takes out a KEY RING and inserts one into the lock.

The DOOR CREAKS OPEN before he can twist it.

He looks back with raised eyebrows. Noelle shakes her head.

> NOELLE (CONT'D)
> So cliché...

INT. DR. BASWELL'S FOYER - CONTINUOUS

Paul steps in and peers around. Noelle remains at the threshold, looking in.

Sparkles of light from the TINKLING chandelier flicker over OIL PAINTINGS of pastoral settings and long-dead Victorians. Brass wall plates lead up the stairs to a STAINED-GLASS MURAL on the long first riser.

PAUL

Hello...? Mr. Evans?

(silence)

I guess the executor must have forgotten to lock up.

NOELLE

I guess...

She steps in behind him. Grimaces.

NOELLE (CONT'D)

What's that noise?

PAUL

What noise?

But Noelle's already following her ears into—

INT. DR. BASWELL'S SITTING ROOM - CONTINUOUS

She stalks the sound. Paul stands by the door, peering around at the unfinished game of chess on a table, the book shelves, the fireplace, a leather reading chair. He smiles wistfully.

Noelle spots the source of the incessant BEEPING.

An old rotary phone receiver hangs off the edge of an end table, OFF-HOOK TONE blaring. Noelle hurries to it and hangs it up.

NOELLE
Ugh! Is that what phones used to sound like?

PAUL
(ignores her)
I wonder how long it's been off the hook?

NOELLE
Dad, don't say "off the hook."

PAUL
(scowls)
I didn't say it like that.

But Noelle's staring down at his feet. He follows her gaze to a FIREPLACE POKER lying haphazardly on the rug.

The phone, the poker. Something's not right here.

A THUMP from above startles them. Plaster dust falls like snow from the ceiling.

They turn to each other, unease growing.

NOELLE
(whispers)
There's someone in the house...

A fact confirmed by a MAN'S SHRIEK OF TERROR from up the winding staircase, ECHOING throughout the house, met by the stoic oil-paint faces of dead men, women and sheep.

ACT ONE

FADE IN:

INT. DR. BASWELL'S SITTING ROOM - DAY

Another THUMP from upstairs.

Paul puts a finger to his lips, shushing Noelle. He picks up the poker, brandishing it like a weapon.

He points to her, then to the corner by the fireplace.

PAUL
(whispers)
Stay. There.

Frightened, Noelle backs into the corner.

Paul steps out into the—

INT. FOYER - CONTINUOUS

Paul creeps to the carpeted staircase and creeps up. A STEP CREAKS and he freezes.

The stained-glass mural captures his attention, a lush green tree set against a partly-cloudy sky, bare roots hanging.

A SMASH OF GLASS startles him. He dashes to the next floor.

Behind him the stained-glass mural CHANGES: the sky darkens, the clouds scudding, the branches sway and the roots wriggle and reach like tentacles.

Paul sees the DAYLIGHT SHIFT on the carpeted stairs at his feet. He whips around to look.

The mural remains unchanged. Disturbed, he rises the last steps.

INT. SECOND FLOOR HALL - CONTINUOUS

The stairs lead to a long hall lined by closed doors, dimly lit by the mural.

                    MAN'S VOICE
               Goodness! My goodness!

A door CREAKS open, allowing more light into the corridor.

Paul heads toward it cautiously, fireplace poker raised in a death-grip. He flinches as his shoes CREAK on the floorboards.

He reaches out to push against the door.

Suddenly it TEARS OPEN.

Paul leaps back as a WILD-HAIRED MAN in a three-piece suit stumbles out, lip bloody, hugging the fireplace shovel.

WILD-HAIRED MAN
The creature—did you see it?

PAUL
What creature?

WILD-HAIRED MAN
Oh, the filthy thing! I cornered it. It leapt. It leapt
right into my hair!

The Wild-Haired Man peers around with bird-like jerkiness.

PAUL
(lowering the poker)
Okay, it's okay. Just relax. Take a deep breath in your
nose... and out through the mouth.

Paul demonstrates. The Wild-Haired Man mimics him. He takes another and another until he's practically hyperventilating.

PAUL (CONT'D)
Forget it. Let's begin with who you are, and why
you're in Dr. Baswell's house.

The Wild-Haired Man TITTERS nervously.

WILD-HAIRED MAN
I'm Marty Evans. The executor of Timothy's estate. I
handle probate mostly, some realty.

MARTY EVANS (the Wild-Haired Man) gives Paul a
pleading look.

MARTY EVANS (CONT'D)
It could still be here.

PAUL
Mr. Evans, I'm Dr. Paul Darling, Timothy's friend
from Baltimore. You say there's a 'creature'...?

MARTY EVANS
Horrible thing, filthy thing.

PAUL
Is it a bat? A rodent?

Marty looks at him as if Paul's the crazy one. He shoots
another frightened look down the hall.

MARTY EVANS
It... I believe it was something not of this—

PAUL
Not of this...?

NOELLE
(calling up)
Dad? Who are you talking to?

PAUL
Everything's fine, hon. Mr. Evans, the estate lawyer,
he chased a squirrel out of the house. Isn't that right?
Noelle rises above the second floor landing. She sees
them standing there, Paul with the poker, Marty
Evans with the shovel, tense and wild-eyed.

MARTY EVANS
A squirrel?

Paul nods. Marty Evans also nods, as if to convince himself.

MARTY EVANS (CONT'D)
A squirrel, yes. Not the black kind. Red. Quite red.
(shudders)
Horrible, nattering thing.
(to Noelle)
It leapt into my hair!

NOELLE
You can hardly tell.
(a "yeah right" look)
Okay if I pick a room, Dad?

PAUL

Go ahead. If there's one with a fireplace, I call dibs.

NOELLE

You can't call dibs.

PAUL

I just did.

Noelle sneers jokingly at him and continues down the hall.

INT. MIDWIFE'S QUARTERS - CONTINUOUS

Noelle steps in and surveys the room. The decor hasn't changed since the 19th century. A bassinet, a GRAMO-PHONE, a four-poster bed, and ugly little porcelain DOLLS.

NOELLE

Creepy... I like it.

She tosses her bag on the bed. UNZIPS it, grabs a handful of clothes and chucks them on the covers.

A bottle of PILLS RATTLES out onto the mattress. She picks them up and turns them over to the label:

ALEXANDRA DARLING

CLOZAPINE 50mg

TAKE AS PRESCRIBED

DRIP! ... DRIP!

Suddenly worried, Noelle turns toward the en suite bathroom, where the DRIPPING WATER grows louder.

INT. KITCHEN - CONTINUOUS

A KETTLE WHISTLES on the stove in this cozy little kitchen. Very clean, late-'60s style, pea green formica and dark wood. Cubed glass in the back door window.

Paul plops a tea bag into a mug and approaches Marty Evans, who's still hugging the fireplace shovel at the table.

Paul sets the mug down and tries to take the shovel from him. Marty jerks it away.

PAUL
Mr. Evans, whatever you think you saw... it isn't
here now.

Paul tugs on the shovel. With one last feeble pullback, Marty lets go. Paul places it between them on the table and sits.

PAUL (CONT'D)
Have some tea. It's chamomile. It'll help calm your
nerves.

Marty nods. He picks it up in both hands and blows on it.

PAUL (CONT'D)
Mr. Evans, does this house have a pest problem?

MARTY EVANS
"Pest."
(stares into his tea)
This place is *haunted*.

INT. MIDWIFE'S QUARTERS - CONTINUOUS

Noelle continues toward the en suite bathroom, the door open a crack. Water DRIPS from inside.

PAUL (V.O.)
You think this house is haunted.

MARTY EVANS (V.O.)
This *town*, Dr. Darling. This whole town is haunted. Ever since Dr. Baswell disappeared. And I, for one, won't sit idly by as it sinks into the abyss!

The SQUEAK of wet skin against porcelain. Noelle hesitates, fingers nearly touching the door.

WATER RIPPLES, as if someone's moving in the tub. Then a GURGLE as that same someone pulled the plug. The TUB DRAINS.

NOELLE
Hello...?

Noelle gently pushes on the door, stiffening when it CREAKS.

PAUL (V.O.)
Mr. Evans, what was it you thought you saw in here?

INT. KITCHEN - CONTINUOUS

Marty throws on his jacket and stands, clearly terrified.

MARTY EVANS
Thank you for the tea. I'm sure you and your
daughter will be very happy here.

He opens the back door.

PAUL
Mr. Evans...?

Marty half-turns. He won't make eye contact.

MARTY EVANS
Please... *I'd rather not speak its name.*

And he scurries out, closing the door behind himself.

Paul sighs. He picks up the shovel by the blade, pulling a disgusted face when he notices slick red smearing his fingertips. He wipes them on a towel and examines the shovel closer. Sees nasty bits of gristle and hair on the blade.

Paul looks toward the hall and the stairs, worried now.

INT. MIDWIFE'S QUARTERS - CONTINUOUS

The door CREAKS open the rest of the way, revealing a small, neat bathroom with a pull-chain flush toilet.

A frosted white curtain surrounds the clawfoot tub. A DARK SHAPE moves behind it, as if someone's sitting in the tub.

> NOELLE
> (not likely)
> Dr. Baswell...?

No sound but the GURGLE of the drain. Noelle takes a hesitant step forward.

A WHIMPER stops her. The whimper of a CRYING WOMAN.

NOELLE'S FLASHBACK: *A different tub, different curtain. A WOMAN'S ARM flops over the edge, wedding ring on the hand, a bottle of pills in it. The pills fall on the wet rug.*

BACK TO SCENE

Noelle's suddenly white as a sheet.

> NOELLE (CONT'D)
> *Mom...?*

A DOOR CHIME rings throughout the house, startling her.

INT. FOYER - CONTINUOUS

Paul enters, glancing into the sitting room as he crosses to the door.

He opens it. SHERIFF CASSIE MALENFANT stands on the porch, mid-30s, dark blue uniform, smudges of dirt on her face and grass in her hair.

> PAUL
> Can I help you, Officer?

> CASSIE
> Sheriff'll do fine. You're Dr. Darling, is that right?

> PAUL
> Just Paul.

> CASSIE
> Just Paul then. I'm Cassie.

Sheriff Malenfant sticks out a dirty hand. Paul hesitates a moment, then shakes it.

> PAUL
> Please, come in.

The Sheriff strides right through the foyer. She peers into the sitting room, then heads for the kitchen. Paul follows.

> CASSIE
> Marty Evans sure blew out of here in a hurry.

PAUL
I think he said he had errands to run?

CASSIE
Are you asking me if he had errands to run?
(off his confusion)
You said it like it was a question.

PAUL
He said he had errands. Is this an interrogation,
Sheriff?

CASSIE
Marty's lip was bloodied. And it looked as if he'd just
seen the Ghost of Christmas Past.

PAUL
Wasn't Future supposed to be the scary one?

CASSIE
Maybe where you're from.

Cassie enters the—

INT. KITCHEN - CONTINUOUS

The Sheriff sees the shovel on the table, the blood and gristle.
Blood staining the crumpled towel on the counter. She turns
to Paul with a quizzical look.

PAUL

The man's delusional. Saying something about a
creature—

CASSIE

Does the blood on this shovel belong to this alleged
creature, or to Marty?

PAUL

It. I suppose.

CASSIE

Then why do you assume he's having delusions?

PAUL

He spoke as if whatever it was... wasn't "of this
world."

CASSIE

And you're convinced he's wrong?

Paul tries to judge whether or not she's serious. He laughs.

PAUL

Of course, I'm sure.

CASSIE

(a grim smile)

Just wanted to be sure we're on the same page. Seems
there's a shortage of level-headed folks in Dark Pines
these days.

Paul picks up the towel gingerly and drops it in the trash bin. He puts the shovel in the sink, blade-first, and begins washing it.

PAUL

I guess I'm not so sure what you mean, Sheriff.

CASSIE

Since Doc Baswell... let's say *disappeared*... the number of odd "disturbances" has jumped exponentially. I don't want to say these events might be psychic in nature, but nothing else fits.

Paul ties up the garbage bag, empty aside from the towel. He starts obsessively scrubbing the table.

PAUL
(skeptical)
"Psychic."

CASSIE

Of the mind? Mental? I'm not the crazy one, Doc. Folks in Dark Pines are losing their marbles at the moment, one by one. Something in the water, I guess.

PAUL

Marty Evans seems to believe the whole town is haunted.

CASSIE

That makes two of us.
(re: the table)
I think it's clean.

Paul stops scrubbing, reopens the trash bag, puts the dirty rag inside and ties it up while Cassie continues.

CASSIE (CONT'D)

I'm not saying it's ghosts. Let's say "mental distress."
The *other* kind of haunted. Look, the reason I
dropped by is to ask for your help. There's a boy
whose friend vanished at the lake.

PAUL

Another disappearance.

CASSIE

Welcome to Dark Pines. Thing is, he won't talk. Not
to me, not to anyone. It's like he's shut down.
Something he witnessed, maybe. Whatever the
reason, I need to speak with him if I'm to find out
what happened to that girl—

PAUL

I'd be happy to help, Sheriff.

CASSIE

I appreciate that. And after we find her, I'd be
derelict in my duties as a peace officer if I didn't urge
you and yours to proceed to the nearest highway on-
ramp.

Noelle SCREAMS from upstairs.

Paul and Cassie share an anxious look and hurry out.

INT. FOYER - MOMENTS LATER

They tear up the stairs, Paul following in Cassie's footsteps as she SNAPS open her hip holster.

> PAUL
> Noelle!

INT. SECOND FLOOR HALL - CONTINUOUS

Another SCREAM as they TRUNDLE down the corridor.

INT. MIDWIFE'S QUARTERS - CONTINUOUS

Cassie enters, drawing her sidearm. Paul rushes in after her.

> PAUL
> Hon?

> NOELLE (O.S.)
> Dad...? There's something in here...!

Cassie moves first, but Paul grabs her shoulder. His look tells her he needs to go alone. Cassie nods and stays put as he approaches the bathroom.

> PAUL
> Noelle? I'm coming in, okay?

He finds Noelle standing in the corner, behind the doorjamb.

PAUL (CONT'D)
What's wrong, honey?

NOELLE
I heard crying. Someone was behind the curtain. I
thought it was—I thought...

She breaks down weeping and grabs Paul. He hugs her
fiercely.

PAUL
I know. It's okay.

NOELLE
It wasn't her. It wasn't her, but it *was* her. Her pills
were in my bag, Dad! What were they doing in my
bag?!

Paul looks out at the bag on the bed. Sees some scattered
clothes but no pills.

PAUL
Your mom's pills? Why would you *bring* those here,
Noelle?

NOELLE
I didn't! I left them at home, I swear! In the bathroom
where she—

NOELLE (CONT'D)
But I saw her *right there!* It was just like when... Dad,
am I going crazy?

Paul locks eyes with Cassie over Noelle's shoulder. Long
enough for her to react to his pain. Then he looks off.

PAUL
You're not crazy, Noelle.
(beat)
I'm going to go look in the tub, okay?

Noelle nods. He lets her go and turns to the bathtub. The
drain GURGLES. He steps toward it.

Cassie looks on from the bedroom. Noelle watches, anxious.

Paul's foot SQUELCHES on the bath mat. He stops and
looks down, troubled. Then he peers into the tub. What he
sees makes him grip the edge of the sink to steady himself.

CASSIE (O.S.)
What is it, Doc?

It's a WEDDING RING, the same ring we saw earlier.

PAUL'S FLASHBACK: *ALEXANDRA DARLING, late-
20s, radiant smile in her wedding gown as Paul slips the ring
on her finger.*

*Their left hands intertwined. Laughter under shimmering
white satin sheets in the bright morning sun.*

Under hot white track lights, the CORONER *hands Paul an* EVIDENCE BAG, *the ring inside. Paul takes it, his grief a gaping wound.*

BACK TO SCENE

Paul holds back a flood of emotion.

> PAUL
> Nothing. It's nothing.

He takes in a deep breath through his nose, then turns and steps away, leaving the WEDDING RING in the bottom of the tub.

With a forced smile, he ushers Noelle out of the bathroom and shuts the door behind them.

The drain GURGLES.

> SLAM TO BLACK.

ACT TWO

FADE IN:

INT./EXT. PAUL'S HYBRID (MOVING) - DAY

Paul and Noelle drive through the QUAINT DOWN-TOWN in silence. The Sheriff's black and white Chevy

Tahoe leads the way.

PEDESTRIANS turn to watch them go. No menace, just curiosity.

PAUL
What you saw in the house, that was just nerves,
okay? You were worked up. From the trip. From Mr.
Evans's agitation.

NOELLE
(unconvinced)
I know, Dad.

PAUL
Everything's going to be okay. All right?

Noelle nods, not making eye contact. Then:

NOELLE
But why did we have to *move*? We could have gotten
another place in Baltimore if all you wanted was to
get out of that house. A bungalow in Franklintown, a
condo...

PAUL
We're not *running away*, Noelle. This is something I
needed to do. I owe a lot to Dr. Baswell. You know he
introduced your mother and me, don't you?

NOELLE
Mom never told me that.

> PAUL
> Well, he did.

> NOELLE
> (considers it)
> But he's dead now.

Paul eyes her.

> PAUL
> We don't know that. And anyway, that doesn't matter. You make a promise to someone, you follow through. Even if they are dead. *Especially* if they're dead.

Noelle gives him a concerned look. He's got a white-knuckled grip on the wheel, staring straight ahead.

EXT. THE O'BRIEN HOUSE - DAY

A door, peeled gray paint, rusty knob. The LOCK TURNS. It opens on an unsmiling MR. O'BRIEN, a lanky, mid-40s man in mechanic's bib coveralls. The door chain cuts a slash across his face.

Paul and Cassie stand on the porch. Broken patio furniture and dead leaves litter the rotted porch boards.

> MR. O'BRIEN
> Breen won't talk, Sheriff. And even if he could I wouldn't let him talk to you.

CASSIE
Craig, if we could just have a moment—

MR. O'BRIEN
Don't "Craig" me, Sheriff. After the way you handled
Carolyn's—
(almost breaks up)
—*accident*, I got nothing to say to you, neither.

CASSIE
The investigation is ongoing—

O'Brien jerks the door open. Paul sees Breen standing
nervous in the background, near the stairs.

MR. O'BRIEN
An investigation that cost me my damn business!
Now I'm gonna say good day to you folks because
that's the way I was raised, but I sure as hell don't
mean it!
(tear-rimmed eyes staring daggers)
Good day, Sheriff. Mister.

And he SLAMS the door. Paul turns to Cassie in the silence
that follows.

CASSIE
I'm sorry about that, Paul. His wife died in a car
crash a few months back. There's still some
irregularities we're looking into, but—

PAUL

It seems like he's made up his mind who's to blame.

CASSIE

Right.

EXT. THE O'BRIENS' STREET - CONTINUOUS

They head back to the Hybrid, parked behind the Sheriff's Tahoe. Noelle's in the front seat. When she sees them, she opens the door, concerned.

NOELLE

What happened?

PAUL

He won't let us speak to him.

NOELLE

So you're just gonna give up?

CASSIE

We've got several pokers in the fire—

NOELLE

Let me do it.

PAUL

Noelle, I don't want you getting involved—

NOELLE

Dad, there's a girl out there who's life could be in danger, and you're gonna give up because some hillbilly won't let you talk to his kid?

PAUL

I knew this was a mistake. I shouldn't have brought you.

CASSIE

She does makes a good point, Paul. What have you got in mind, girl?

EXT. THE O'BRIEN HOUSE – DAY

The front door bursts open. Mr. O'Brien blocks the doorway, fuming. He brightens somewhat at what he sees.

MR. O'BRIEN

Can I help you, young lady?

Noelle stands at the door, one headphone in, holding her phone and a bunch of PAPERS.

NOELLE

I'm a friend of Breen's.
(re: the papers)
I brought his homework?

Mr. O'Brien looks at the papers. He peers out at the empty street, then again at Noelle. Finally, he lets her in.

INTERCUT INT. PAUL'S HYBRID/INT. THE
O'BRIEN HOUSE - DAY

Paul and Cassie sit in the front seats, intent on Paul's CELL
PHONE on the dash, showing the inside of the O'Brien
house via Noelle's cell.

> NOELLE (O.S.)
> You have a nice home, Mr. O'Brien.

> MR. O'BRIEN (O.S.)
> Thank you. Used to be nicer, when the missus was
> among us.

Noelle fakes a smile. Hoarders have got nothing on this
place.

Dust motes dance over garbage bags, bills, newspapers and
liquor bottles. Dirty laundry trails down the stairs. Breen
stands at the top. He smiles, unsure.

> MR. O'BRIEN (CONT'D)
> This young lady brought your homework.

> NOELLE
> Hey, Breen.

> MR. O'BRIEN
> Well? Ain't you gonna say something?

Breen struggles.

BREEN
Thank you.

Noelle startles at hearing him speak. In the car, Paul and
Cassie share a look of shock.

CASSIE
Faking it the whole time. The little sneak.

MR. O'BRIEN
Now if anyone in class asks you if Breen said
anything, you'll tell them he was as quiet as a dog
fart, won't ya?

NOELLE
(grimaces)
I'll just say I slipped it under the door.

PAUL
Noelle, I want you to look for anything suspicious,
okay? Anything out of place.

NOELLE
Duh.

MR. O'BRIEN
(calling up)
What's that, kiddo?

NOELLE
Just, uh... listening to a podcast.

Mr. O'Brien appears confused. He shrugs and wanders off through the junk toward another room. The TV comes on a moment later to CAVALRY TRUMPETS and PISTOLS.

Breen's smile fades, his eyes narrowing.

> BREEN
> Who are you, really?

> NOELLE
> I'm Noelle. My dad's a shrink.

> PAUL
> Don't say "shrink," hon—

> BREEN
> I don't need a psychiatrist.

> NOELLE
> Sheriff Cassie wants him to talk to you, but since she blew his cover, they asked me to try.

> BREEN
> Are they listening right now?

Noelle nods.

> BREEN
> What do you want? I don't remember anything. Why don't you people leave me alone?

PAUL

Noelle, if you really want to help, you're going to
have to talk about your mom.

NOELLE

Do I have to?

PAUL

You don't have to do anything you don't want to,
honey. You knew this would be difficult. But it was
your idea, remember?

BREEN

What's he saying?

PAUL

Be strong, okay? You were right, it's the quickest way
to get to him. We may not have much time.

NOELLE

Okay. Okay. But I'm gonna need a new phone if
we're gonna keep doing this.

CASSIE

Oh, she's good.

Paul nods, unable to deny it.

NOELLE

(to Breen)

Your mom died a little while ago, didn't she?

NOELLE (CONT'D)
(off Breen's nod)
I know what it's like to lose someone you love. My
mom died, too. Almost a year ago. I was the one who
found her.

Cassie turns to Paul. He stares straight ahead again, the
wheel gripped tightly.

NOELLE (CONT'D)
Sheriff Cassie says any little detail you can give us
will help. You want to save your friend, don't you?

PAUL
Sarah. Her name is Sarah. Say her name, honey.

NOELLE
Dad! Quit buzzing in my ear!
(to Breen)
We want to help find Sarah, Breen. Will you help us?

Finally, the boy nods.

NOELLE (CONT'D)
Good. We're gonna find her, Breen, okay? I promise.

CASSIE
She's a natural.

Paul's grip on the wheel loosens.

PAUL
She takes after her mother.

INTERCUT INT. PAUL'S HYBRID/INT. BREEN'S
ROOM - CONTINUOUS

As Breen heads for his bed, Noelle looks around.

Posters of metal bands on the walls. Comics like "Weird
Tales" and "Vault of Horror," and monster figurines stacked
everywhere else. Black strips of cloth hang from the ceiling
fan. A PAINTING OF A SQUID-FACED MONSTER
hangs over the bed.

NOELLE
Cool painting.

BREEN
Sarah did it for me.

PAUL (O.S.)
Turn the phone, hon. I need to speak to Breen face-
to-face.

NOELLE
My dad wants to talk to you, okay?

Breen nods. She takes out the earbud and turns the phone so
Paul and Breen can see each other.

PAUL
Hi, Breen. I'm Paul.

> BREEN
> Yeah, hi.

> PAUL
> Was it your father's idea to stop talking?

> BREEN
> It was mine. My dad only went along with it because
> the truth is worse.
> (grave)
> The truth is way worse.

> PAUL
> What is the truth, Breen?

Breen looks off. Swallows audibly.

> BREEN
> If I tell you, you'll think I'm crazy.

> NOELLE
> Believe me, he will *not* think you're crazy.

> BREEN
> (considers; then)
> After my mom's funeral, Sarah came around the
> house a lot. Asking if I was okay, if I needed
> anything. I thought it was weird. We never talked
> before in school. Never even said hi. And suddenly
> she's coming by every day, bringing me and Dad
> home-baked cookies and books on grieving.

PAUL

Like she was trying to make up for something.

BREEN

That's what I thought. It was awkward at first, but pretty soon we made friends. We listen to the same music, we both like fishing. But then, a few weeks ago, Sarah decided to confess.

PAUL

Confess?

BREEN

She's the reason my mom died.

Paul and Cassie share a surprised look.

BREEN (CONT'D)

I was sick the day my Mom died. She went to get chicken soup for me. She always made me soup when I was sick.

NOELLE

My mom used to bake pie.

Breen tries to smile.

BREEN

I asked her to check out a book from the library while she was out. This book...

Breen picks up a BLACK BOOK from his roll-top desk, a pentagram and a single word in white on the cover: *NECRO-NOMICON*.

> PAUL
> I can't see the title.

> NOELLE
> It's the *Necronomicon*, Dad. The Book of the Dead.

Breen fights back tears. One falls, then another.

> BREEN
> When Sarah told me what really happened that day,
> I was so angry.

BREEN'S FLASHBACK: *By a DIRT ROAD, Sarah squeezes through thorny branches, plucking RASPBERRIES and plopping them into her mouth.*

She spots a large, blood-red berry, big as a plum. She can't believe her luck. But it's near the edge of the hill.

> BREEN (V.O.)
> Sarah was picking road berries. Raspberries,
> blackberries, they grow best along dirt roads. We call
> them road berries. They always taste the sweetest.

MRS. O'BRIEN, a pleasant-looking woman in her late-40s, drives the dirt road in a beat-up station wagon, humming tonelessly, GROCERIES in the passenger seat.

Sarah reaches out, reaches... She almost has it when the ground gives way. Stumbling, she reaches out blindly, pitching forward... down the hill...

The station wagon comes over a rise...

Sarah lurches out into the road, falling to her hands and knees just as Mrs. O'Brien takes the corner.

BREEN (V.O.)

It was an accident. Just bad timing. That's all.

Sarah's and Mrs. O'Brien's eyes meet, wide from shock.

Mrs. O'Brien cranks the wheel. The wagon tears off hard right, over the ditch.

Sarah covers her eyes at the CRUNCH OF STEEL AND GLASS.

BACK TO SCENE

PAUL

I'm sorry, Breen. Take a moment, if you need it.

BREEN

I'm fine.
(deep breath)

When my Dad got the car back, after they'd washed out all the blood, they found this book mixed up with all the groceries.

BREEN (CONT'D)

When Sarah told me what happened, even though it
wasn't her fault, even though she felt so bad she'd
spent the next three months making up for it, all I
could think of was this book in the wreck of my
mom's car that she got because of me. And all I
wanted was to make Sarah pay. I'd read about the
spells in the *Necronomicon*. I never thought they
would really work. I guess maybe I just did it to make
me feel better.

PAUL

That's natural. Cathartic.

BREEN'S FLASHBACK: *He sits in a CHALK PENTA-
GRAM on the floor, each point marked by a BLACK
CANDLE, the book in his lap.*

BREEN (V.O.)

I went to the attic. Dad was at his A.A. meeting. I
was alone.

*Breen reads the book aloud, lips struggling to form difficult
words. The CANDLES FLICKER, throwing shadows over
the room.*

*He continues, nervous yet forceful. The attic door's open on
the lighted hallway.*

BREEN (V.O.) (CONT'D)

I did it! I *called* It! I swear I didn't think anything
would happen...

Suddenly, the DOOR SLAMS SHUT and the CANDLES FIZZLE OUT, throwing Breen into pitch dark.

BACK TO SCENE

Breen grips the book in terror, remembering everything. Noelle watches him, trying to hide her own fear.

> BREEN (CONT'D)
> We went fishing the very next day, we acted like nothing happened. We even had fun. I almost forgot all about the day before. But then, out on the lake—
> (through tears)
> —*It* came. It was the most horrible *Thing* I'd ever seen. And It took Sarah. There was nothing I could do to help her!

> PAUL
> What, Breen? What took her?

> BREEN
> The book calls him "the Great Dreamer."

Breen looks up through his tears and points. Noelle follows his gaze to the SQUID-FACED MONSTER from Sarah's painting.

> BREEN (CONT'D)
> *Cthulhu* took her.

SLAM TO BLACK.

ACT THREE

FADE IN:

INT. DINER - DAY

The place could be '50s-retro or it hasn't changed since then. A handful of CUSTOMERS this afternoon. The kind-faced, mid-40s WAITRESS chats with a table of OLD LADIES. Cassie, Paul and Noelle sit at a booth, having coffee and eating lunch.

CASSIE

Can you make any sense of it?

PAUL

Well there's no "Cthulhu," that much is obvious. The trauma of Sarah falling in the lake, splashing around, his inability to help her. His imagination must have filled in the details. Cthulhu, the *Necro*—whatever.

NOELLE

—*Nomicon*, Dad. *Necronomicon*.

PAUL

The book was fresh in his mind from the night before, so...

CASSIE

You're saying his mind created the tentacles of this...
Cthulhu thing? What the hell is a Cthulhu, anyway?

Noelle shrugs, eating her pie.

PAUL

It was the tentacle part that sold me on the idea.
Tentacles often symbolize dangers lurking in the
deep, or in this case, the subconscious. These
tentacles literally *dragged* Sarah into the water, into
her subconscious, to deal with what she'd been afraid
to confront: Breen's mother's death. I see this all the
time in my practice. It's usually ghosts or aliens—but
ghosts, aliens, Cthulhu... they're all just the products
of overactive imaginations struggling to deal with
very real traumas.

CASSIE

Okay. But what I want to know is, did Breen conjure
up those tentacles to justify his inaction, or to cover
up a murder?

They stare at each other in silence.

The BELL DINGS over the door and a CRAZED MAN
bursts in, startling everyone.

CRAZED MAN
*IT'S THE RADIOS! THE RADIOS, THE
RADIOS, THE RADIOS!*

He STOMPS over to the closest booth where the old ladies sit, and tries to yank the JUKEBOX from the partition wall.

Noelle eats her pie throughout, interested but hungry. Cassie calmly wipes her mouth with her napkin.

PAUL
What's going on?

CASSIE
That's Reggie Walsh. Who you might call the town drunk, if your town didn't have as many drunks as Dark Pines.

The Waitress approaches the Crazed Man (REGGIE WALSH).

WAITRESS
Now calm down, Reg. Let that thing go. It didn't do nothin' to you.

Reggie loosens his grip on the jukebox but doesn't let go.

REGGIE WALSH
If you heard what I heard, you wouldn't say that.
(to the customers)
You'd all be tearing out your radios, or jamming a damn fork in your ears! Right!

Reggie lets go of the jukebox and grabs an old woman's fork off her plate. The women gasp.

Paul sees Cassie calmly reach for her TASER.

The Waitress lays a hand on Reggie's, the one holding the knife, firm but friendly.

> WAITRESS
> These aren't even radios, Reg. They're miniature jukes. You remember jukes, don'tcha, Reg?

He looks at her hand on his. Sees the jukeboxes in the other booths. He calms and drops the fork on the table.

> REGGIE WALSH
> Jukeboxes. No FM band, no AM band. No signals in the airwaves.

> WAITRESS
> That's right. Let's get you a cup of coffee, Reg. We can talk all about the radios, if you want.

Reginald nods shakily. The Waitress leads him to a table.

Cassie SNAPS her holster closed, lets out a breath.

The Waitress passes by their table on the way to the coffee carafes. She shrugs at Cassie.

> WAITRESS (CONT'D)
> Something in the water.

Paul nods, looking like he's coming to a conclusion.

NOELLE
(mouth full)
Maybe the tentacles were real... like... Ogopogo or
the Loch Ness monster? What if it's a giant squid left
behind from the Cretaceous period?

PAUL
In a freshwater lake. I let you watch too many horror
movies.

NOELLE
I'm just spit-balling, Dad! Do you guys really think a
little kid like Breen could've done that? Push his best
friend into the water and—what? Just watched her
drown?

CASSIE
He has the motive. You heard his story. Sarah caused
his mother's death. Inadvertently or not...

PAUL
I can't see it. His expressions, his speech patterns...
he seemed genuinely upset.

Noelle agrees with a nod.

CASSIE
So did the Menendez brothers. Upset could mean
anything, Paul. It could mean he regrets letting her
drown just as easy as pushing her in.

PAUL
Maybe...

CASSIE
Either way you slice it, Sarah is in that lake. We can't
prove Breen innocent or guilty until we find her
body.

EXT. DEEP BOG LAKE - EVENING

A YOUNG DIVER sits on the edge of a dock. She spits into
the mask, rubs it around, then puts it on.

She plunges into water the color of tea. Fins kicking, eyes
sweeping back and forth.

A kitchen sink rots at the bottom of the lake. A smallmouth
bass swims out from behind a rusty propane tank.

She grabs a tree stump, pulling herself along.

On the surface, Marty Evans and HECTOR EVANS (a
skinny, balding version of his brother) haul in a NET filled
with sticks and rotted leaves.

On the shore, DEPUTY LAWSON, a big, beefy guy in his
late-20s with a wide-brimmed hat, sips coffee from a
Thermos lid.

Leaving her Tahoe, Cassie trudges through the muck to his
side.

                           CASSIE
                  How's the dredge going, Ray?

                      DEPUTY LAWSON
          Looks like Pines County's got itself yet another
          unofficial garbage dump. The O'Brien boy give ya
                     anything to work with yet?

                           CASSIE
          Spilled his guts. I'll fill you in back at the shop.

Deputy Lawson nods, satisfied with that.

Something pale gleams at the bottom of the lake.

The Diver swipes away muck. Reveals a HUMAN FOOT.
Bubbles explode from her mouth as she screams.

                      MARTY EVANS (O.S.)
                   Sheriff! We've found something!

Cassie and the deputy look out.

INT. MRS. PETERSON'S LIVING ROOM - EVENING

Almost every surface has neatly-arranged ceramics or
vibrant, visceral PAINTINGS on it. On the table sits a set of
Russian nesting dolls with realistic paintings of the Peterson
family: the biggest a smiling late-30s man with a goatee, MR.
PETERSON; the next smaller a Mrs. Peterson doll; the
smallest, Sarah's.

On the sofa, Paul picks up the Sarah doll and smiles.

MRS. PETERSON enters with a coffee tray, a frazzled, hippyish woman in her early-40s. Paul hastily puts the Sarah doll down.

MRS. PETERSON
Jack—my husband—made those.

PAUL
They're cute. Is Mr. Peterson...?

She sets the coffees down. Paul takes his.

MRS. PETERSON
He left the two of us little over a year ago.

PAUL
I'm sorry to hear that.

MRS. PETERSON
Don't be. He was notoriously unreliable. We used to
joke he had an "artistic temperament." Once he'd
skipped out in the middle of dinner. But he'd usually
be back within a day or so, a week at the most. This
last time, he just never came back.

PAUL
(curiosity piqued)
He disappeared?

MRS. PETERSON
I wouldn't say that. Just left.

PAUL
I can't imagine anyone wanting to leave this house.
It's so vibrant.

MRS. PETERSON
We're a family of artists. Music is my gift. *Was*, I
should say. I don't find much use for it now Sarah's
gone.

PAUL
I understand Sarah's a painter.

MRS. PETERSON
That's right. I know it sounds like something out of a
Disney movie, but at times it felt as though her
paintings just might come alive and leap off the
canvas. It's silly.

PAUL
It doesn't sound silly at all.

Mrs. Peterson smiles. She sips her coffee.

MRS. PETERSON
Martin Evans went wild over her work. He calls
himself—what was it? An *aficionado*. He even held
an exhibit. Of course, he ended up buying most of
her paintings himself, but a few of her best ones sold
to people from away.

PAUL

She's very talented.

(then)

Did Sarah ever speak to you about Carolyn O'Brien?

MRS. PETERSON

Lynn? No. No, I don't think so.

PAUL

Apparently, Sarah told Breen she was there the day
of the accident. That she may have accidentally
caused it.

Distraught, Mrs. Peterson picks up her coffee and sets it back
down. She looks back at the piano and easel, taking up much
of the next room.

MRS. PETERSON

I told her not to tell the police.

PAUL

You did.

MRS. PETERSON

What purpose would it serve? It was an accident.
Accident's happen all the time.

PAUL

Did Sarah express feelings of guilt or remorse to you?
Did she behave any differently? Did she... seem
depressed, or anxious?

MRS. PETERSON
(considers it)
A few weeks after the accident, Sarah began
complaining that her stomach hurt. Of course, I took
her to the naturopath. He prescribed a total cleanse,
followed by a gluten-free diet. It worked for a while.
Then the headaches started.

PAUL
Internalized anxiety or guilt often manifests as
physical pain. Intestinal, joints, headaches.

MRS. PETERSON
And here I was so certain that awful school cafeteria
was the problem.
(beat)
If Sarah was troubled, why wouldn't she have
told me?

PAUL
Kids her age, they start to pull away. They don't
always tell you what's on their minds like they
used to.

MRS. PETERSON
Do you have children, Paul?

PAUL
(nods)
A girl. A year or two older than yours.

                    MRS. PETERSON
            And does she tell you what's on her mind?

                        PAUL
        I'm a psychologist. Of course, she doesn't. The trick is
                    to learn how to listen.
                      (considers)
        We're going to find your daughter, Mrs. Peterson.
        Mrs. Peterson smiles and lays a hand on Paul's.

                    MRS. PETERSON
            I know. I dreamed you would. I only now just
                realized it was you I'd dreamt of.

Paul hides his disbelief behind a smile.

EXT. DEEP BOG LAKE - EVENING

HUMAN REMAINS slump to the shore, wrapped in
the net.

Marty and Hector Evans wipe their hands off on their pants
with a weary look at each other.

The Diver sits shivering on a log, huddled under a blanket.

DR. EMMETT PROCTOR, a jovial, bearded man in his
late-60s, rolls the corpse over.

Cassie and Deputy Lawson await, anxious and slightly
nauseated.

Doc Proctor removes the net with gloved hands.

The MAN's face is a wet mask of terror. Waxy gray flesh, eyes sunken, mouth frozen in a rictus. A familiar goatee.

                    CASSIE
          I think I recognize him.

                 DOC PROCTOR
          It's Jack Peterson... The sculptor.

               DEPUTY LAWSON
     Sarah's pop? Didn't he skip town a last year?

                 DOC PROCTOR
     Indeed. And it would appear this time he's come
     back for good. Only it won't be a happy reunion.

INT. DR. BASWELL'S HOUSE - MIDWIFE'S QUAR-
TERS - NIGHT

Paul stands in front of the bathtub, hands in his pockets, staring down into the empty basin like a man in a trance.

As if sensing his presence, the drain GURGLES.

PAUL'S FLASHBACK: *Alexandra's hand slung over the edge of the tub as Paul stumbles in and drops to his knees on the damp bath mat among the scattered pills.*

He grabs her hand in his. Hauls her lifeless body out of the water and hugs her. Weeps and rocks her back and forth.

BACK TO SCENE

Paul backs out of the bathroom, beaten, flicking off the light.

> NOELLE
> Dad? What are you doing in my room?

> PAUL
> Checking for bedbugs. All safe.

> NOELLE
> Did you find those pills?

Paul looks innocently at the bed.

> PAUL (CONT'D)
> What pills?

> NOELLE
> (annoyed)
> Mom's pills?

> PAUL
> Maybe the sheriff found them.

She eyes him, suspicious. Then she nods.

> NOELLE
> Maybe. G'night, Dad.

> PAUL
> 'Night, Noley.

Noelle gives him her patented look of aggravation.

PAUL (CONT'D)

Sorry–*Noelle*. Sometimes, I forget you're not a little
girl anymore.

Noelle smiles. He smiles back.

PAUL (CONT'D)

Tomorrow, first light, we'll pack up our things and get
out of here if you want to, okay?

NOELLE

No, Dad. We can't leave until we find Sarah. You
know, a wise man once told me, you make a promise
to someone, you follow through.

PAUL

I bet this guy was pretty handsome, too, wasn't he?

Noelle laughs. Paul grins and shuts the door behind himself.

INT. MASTER BEDROOM - MOMENTS LATER

Another four-poster bed, much larger than Noelle's. A vanity
with an ivory shaving kit and a brass perfume vaporizer.

Paul stands looking at his tired face in the mirror. He
rummages in his pants pocket. He takes out the bottle of pills
and stares at them for a long, hard moment.

ALEXANDRA DARLING
CLOZAPINE 50MG

TAKE AS PRESCRIBED

PAUL'S FLASHBACK: *As Cassie enters the Midwife's Quarters, weapon drawn, Paul spots the pills on the bed. He bends and scoops them up, then puts a hand on Cassie's shoulder to stop her from entering the bathroom.*

PAUL (FLASHBACK)
Noelle? I'm coming in, okay?

BACK TO SCENE

Paul places the pills in a drawer, sighs, and shuts it.

EXT. DOC PROCTOR'S OFFICE – NIGHT

A squat white house with a placard lit by a single spotlight:

DR. E. PROCTOR
GENERAL PRACTITIONER

INT. DOC PROCTOR'S OFFICE - MORGUE - NIGHT

JACK PETERSON'S REMAINS lie on the steel table under the flickering track lighting. Light jazz on a nearby RADIO.

Doc Proctor lifts Jack's eyelids, speaks into a RECORDER.

DOC PROCTOR
Subject appears to have been submerged a day,
maybe less. No immediate signs of drowning...

> DOC PROCTOR (CONT'D)
> No froth around the nose and mouth, no apparent
> hemorrhaging in the sinuses. Will know more once
> I've performed an internal exam.

Doc Proctor runs his finger over a tray full of CORONER'S TOOLS. He selects the scalpel, brings it to the body.

> DOC PROCTOR (CONT'D)
> Preparing to make the first incision.

STATIC interrupts the jazz as he cuts into the Jack's flesh. Doc Proctor backs away, startled and disgusted.

> DOC PROCTOR (CONT'D)
> Oh...! Oh, Lord!

Doc Proctor watches in horror as DARK, VISCOUS LIQUID spews out of the incision, oozing out over the table, onto the floor, the BODY COLLAPSING on itself, the RADIO STATIC growing louder.

Proctor bumps into the table, startles. The radio falls onto the floor, SPLITTING open. The STATIC stops abruptly.

And the morgue drain GURGLES, sucking up the filthy liquid.

INT. DR. BASWELL'S HOUSE - MASTER BEDROOM - NIGHT

In the en suite bathroom, WATER DRIPS. A PUDDLE spills out from under the door and creeps across the floor to the bed.

Paul sleeps soundly, lit by the moon.

At the foot of the bed, the blanket rises, as if to let in an UNSEEN PRESENCE. It ripples, shifting as the presence fills the empty side of the bed.

Paul breathes deeply and rolls over. His eyes come open.

He blinks and jerks back in horror.

ALEXANDRA DARLING, pretty and pale in the moonlight, rises from the pillow...

PAUL
You can't—

She puts a finger to his lips.

ALEXANDRA DARLING
Shhhhh.

She pushes him gently back to the pillow. At first he resists. Then he relents. She climbs on top of him, reaches under the blanket.

He shivers, watching her dark eyes as she moves on top of him. Up and down. Her lips upturned in a smile that doesn't reach her eyes.

PAUL
I've missed you. Alex, I've missed you so much.

Again, she places a finger on his lips. Shushes him.

Her bucking becomes more frenzied. Paul reaches out but doesn't touch her flesh. Afraid to. Tears fall from his eyes. Finally he grasps her behind the head and pulls her to his lips.

They move together, their lips pressed together, until it's obvious Paul has climaxed. A beat passes in silence.

ALEXANDRA DARLING
Don't. Ever. Leave me.

And she pulls away. Her grin widens as she looks down at him–terrified, sweating, breathing heavily–almost with disdain. Then she rolls off, vanishing into darkness as thick as fog.

Paul catches his breath. After a moment turns to her.

The other side of the bed is empty. In the dark, Paul considers the implications. They look grim.

SLAM TO BLACK.

.

ACT FOUR

FADE IN:

INT. DARK PINES SHERIFF'S DEPARTMENT - DAY

Cassie sits behind her desk, sifting through paperwork. Deputy Lawson places a mug of coffee in front of her.

> DEPUTY LAWSON
> You been up all night, Cass, or ya just look like it?

> CASSIE
> Both, I suppose.

She drinks the coffee greedily.

> CASSIE (CONT'D)
> You make a mean cup of joe, Deputy.

> DEPUTY LAWSON
> That's eighty-percent gun oil.

Cassie chuckles.

> DEPUTY LAWSON (CONT'D)
> Told Joanie Peterson the news about her estranged husband.

> CASSIE
> How'd she take it?

DEPUTY LAWSON

Pretty well. She'd gotten a few postcards since he left. Last one was a month ago, from Ohio. No message, no return address.

CASSIE

How did she know they were from Jack?

DEPUTY LAWSON

Damnedest thing. He'd always sign them with a thumbprint on red paint.

CASSIE

That is weird. Sculptor, wasn't he? Maybe it was like a signature. For his pottery.

Deputy Lawson shrugs.

DEPUTY LAWSON

She gave me the last postcard, anyways. I matched it with the prints we took from the D.B.

CASSIE

Good work.

He nods appreciatively.

CASSIE (CONT'D)

So what do we think? He heard about his kid's disappearance, came back to help find her, fell in the lake and drowned?

> DEPUTY LAWSON
> That's my line of thinking.

The DESK PHONE RINGS. Cassie's got her hands full with her coffee. Deputy Lawson picks it up.

> DEPUTY LAWSON (CONT'D)
> (into phone)
> Dark Pines Sheriff's Department, Deputy Lawson spea– Oh, hey, Doc.

He listens to the muted voice.

> DEPUTY LAWSON (CONT'D)
> That is all kinds of messed-up. We'll be right there.

He hangs up and turns to Cassie.

> DEPUTY LAWSON (CONT'D)
> You aren't gonna believe this.

INT. MORGUE - DAY

Cassie and Deputy Lawson look down with disgust at the table covered in crusted dark brown sludge.

> CASSIE
> What are we looking at here, Emmett?

> DOC PROCTOR
> That's your D.B., Jack Peterson. Or *was*, I suppose I should say.

DEPUTY LAWSON
That's decomp juice?

DOC PROCTOR
That's I don't know what. But it *was* him.

CASSIE
What do you mean it was him?

DOC PROCTOR
When I cut into him last night, it appeared as though everything beneath the skin was composed of this... filth.

Cassie and Deputy Lawson look again, skeptical.

DOC PROCTOR (CONT'D)
For a body to decay this much, it would have to have been subjected to sodium hydroxide, otherwise known as lye, for several days, which does leave a mess much like this, like wet coffee grounds.

Cassie sneers at the Thermos of coffee in her hand.

DOC PROCTOR (CONT'D)
But if that were the case, we'd at least have some bone husks to look at.

DEPUTY LAWSON
(shuddering)
"Husks."

DOC PROCTOR

Indeed. Now what you see here are the remains of
the most rapid, efficient human decomposition in
history. If I were an entirely different man, prone to
wild speculation with absolutely no basis in medical
science, I'd say we're looking at the remains of some
sort of pod person.

CASSIE

Pod people...? Any less wacky options, Mulder?

DOC PROCTOR

Something in the water caused this. And if that's the
case, we need to start warning people as quickly as
possible.

Their eyes follow the crusted sludge to where it's pooled
around the floor drain. The drain GURGLES.

INT. DR. BASWELL'S HOUSE - MASTER BEDROOM
- DAY

Paul's under the shower, washing his hair. Soap circles into
the drain at his feet.

He turns off the water. Steps out onto the bath mat.

He rubs condensation from the mirror. Grins at himself, a
skeleton's grin. Dark circles under his eyes.

He sticks his toothbrush under the faucet and turns on the
tap. Brushes his teeth.

He flips the blanket off the mattress to make the bed.

The right side of the bed, which had always been Alexandra's side, seems darker. He touches the fitted sheet. Rubs his fingers together in curiosity.

                    PAUL
                    Damp.

He peers over his shoulder at the bathroom.

INT. KITCHEN - DAY

Noelle sleepily pours water into the coffee machine, turns it on. It GURGLES.

The DOORBELL CHIMES, startling her out of her morning stupor.

INT. MASTER BEDROOM - CONTINUOUS

Paul hears the CHIME echo throughout the house. He pulls on a shirt and heads for the door.

INT. FOYER - MOMENTS LATER

Paul opens the door. Cassie stands on the door mat.

                    CASSIE
            Can I trouble you for a moment?

Noelle steps in behind Paul with a mug of coffee to her lips.

CASSIE (CONT'D)
I'd hold off on drinking that if I were you, hon.

INT. SHERIFF'S TAHOE (MOVING) - DAY

Cassie drives a wooded dirt road. Paul rides shotgun.

CASSIE
You know I just took this job when Sheriff Deacon
retired a month back. Then we get two
disappearances in the span of a few weeks. And now
Dark Pines might have an environmental disaster on
its hands.

PAUL
Everyone's been saying there's something in the
water.

CASSIE
No one ever considered it might be true.

PAUL
At least we don't have to deal with a giant squid.

CASSIE
Frankly, I'd be less anxious if it was.

Cassie grins. Her CELL PHONE RINGS, startling them
both. She thumbs ANSWER. Deputy Lawson responds
OVER SPEAKERPHONE.

CASSIE

Sheriff Malenfant.

DEPUTY LAWSON (V.O.)

Cass, I just got off the horn with Buffalo P.D. You'll never guess what they said.

CASSIE

Not in the mood to play Miss Cleo, Ray.

DEPUTY LAWSON (V.O.)

Jack Peterson? B.P.D. was able to match him from the prints. He had no I.D. when he was found so they couldn't contact the family.

CASSIE

The point, Ray?

DEPUTY LAWSON (V.O.)

Landlord found him in his bachelor apartment three weeks ago, hung from a rafter like that old-timer from *Shawshank*. The movie, not the prison.

CASSIE

The prison's fictional, Ray.

DEPUTY LAWSON (V.O.)

Apparently so is our D.B. If he was dead and buried in Upstate New York, how in the heck did his remains wash up in Dark Pines three weeks later?

Paul and Noelle share a puzzled look.

CASSIE
I wish I knew, Ray. Thanks.

She hangs up. The two of them ride in silence for a beat.

CASSIE (CONT'D)
Well, this case went from strange to outright bonkers
in sixty seconds.

Disturbed, Paul looks off at the blur of trees.

EXT. WATER TREATMENT PLANT - DAY

Overcast sky. CROWS circle a series of low brick buildings
and WATER TOWERS. The sound of RUSHING
WATER in the distance. The Tahoe pulls into a muddy lot
by a drain pond and the sign:

DARK PINES WATER
TREATMENT FACILITY

Cassie and Paul get out. She heads for the long white
stucco building hidden among the trees. Paul follows.

PAUL
You really think Sarah might be here?

CASSIE
We're just going over the same territory at the
dredge. Water draws in and out of here directly from
the lake. If she did drown, this is where we'll find her.

She gestures toward the crows.

                    CASSIE
              Must be feeding time.

                    PAUL
       Crows are carrion eaters, aren't they?

With a grim nod, Cassie draws her sidearm.

INT. DR. BASWELL'S HOUSE - MIDWIFE'S QUAR-
TERS - DAY

Noelle's on the bed bobbing her head to music, reading
Stephen King's *IT*. A THUMP outside her room startles her.
She pulls out an earbud and puts down her book.

                    NOELLE
                     Dad?

INT. SECOND FLOOR HALL - DAY

Noelle creeps down the hall. The sound of RUMMAGING
and hushed CURSES drifts down from above.

She tenses, seeing the ATTIC STAIRS have been pulled
down.

INT. FILTER ANNEX BUILDING - DAY

MACHINERY HUMS. Giant steel pipes snake through the massive, dimly-lit building. Long shadows. Safety sings all over.

The front door opens and Cassie steps in. The Administration Office appears empty when she peeks in the window.

> CASSIE
> Pauline? Anybody here?

Paul enters behind her, pulling a sour face.

> PAUL
> It stinks in here.

> CASSIE
> It's a raw sewage plant. What did you expect?

> PAUL
> Would it kill them to put out some potpourri?

There's a CLANG among the pipes, echoing above the HUM. They turn toward the sound and head away from the office.

Under Pauline's desk, a LEG POKES OUT FROM A POOL OF BLOOD. Blood-spattered pantyhose, socks and running shoes.

> PAUL (O.S.)
> Is this place usually so dead?

> CASSIE
>
> On a weekday, there's at least twenty people on shift.

She makes a sweeping gesture toward the machinery.

> CASSIE
>
> This plant treats the water supply for about about five-thousand homes in Dark Pines and the surrounding communities. Pauline runs the office. If she's not here, Hector Evans, the plant operator, does his best to keep the place going.

> PAUL
>
> Evans?

> CASSIE
>
> Marty's brother.
> (beat)
> *SHERIFF'S DEPARTMENT! ANYBODY HERE?*

Her voice ECHOES back to them.

> CASSIE (CONT'D)
>
> Guess not.

Paul nods. Cassie leads him through the large, snaking pipes.

EXT. WATER TREATMENT PLANT - MOMENTS LATER

Giant paddles churn in the sludge tanks with a HEAVY RUMBLE as Paul and Cassie move between them.

Paul spots a white hard-hat lies in the grass. He follows a walking path to a bush surrounding the tanks. A pair of work boots and smooth legs stick out from the branches.

PAUL
Sheriff...

She follows his look to a DEAD WOMAN nestled in the bush, her face an exploded mess, arms splayed. Cassie grabs her RADIO.

CASSIE
Ray, this is Cass. We're gonna need some backup.
Code ten. Repeat, code ten. Over.

The BLAST of radio STATIC hurts their ears.

INT. DR. BASWELL'S HOUSE - ATTIC - DAY

Noelle creeps nervously up the last few steps. When she sees Marty Evans rummaging in an OLD STEAMER TRUNK she relaxes.

MARTY EVANS
It's in here somewhere, I certain of it!

NOELLE
Mr. Evans?

Marty stiffens. As he slowly turns, his crazed look becomes a cross between a grimace and a smile.

MARTY EVANS
Daughter Darling! What a pleasant surprise!

NOELLE
What are you doing here?

MARTY EVANS
Dr. Baswell was right all along.

Marty reaches into a suit jacket pocket. Noelle tenses as he withdraws the hand. Relaxes again when she sees it's just a handkerchief. He daubs his sweaty forehead with it.

NOELLE
Right about what, Mr. Evans?

MARTY EVANS
You'll see, Daughter Darling. You'll *all* see, soon enough. Then you'll wish you'd heeded the warnings!

With that, he runs headlong toward her. Before Noelle can jump out of his way, he pushes past her and dashes down the stairs.

INT. DR. BASWELL'S FOYER - MOMENTS LATER

Noelle peers out the window as Marty Evans's old Volvo PEELS out of the driveway. She grabs her phone and TEXTS.

EXT. WATER TREATMENT PLANT - DAY

Paul and Cassie crouch-walk alongside large pipes, Deep Bog Lake visible up ahead, past the old brick PUMPING STATION.

A BUZZ makes Paul jump. He stops running and pulls out his cell. It's a text from Noelle.

> PAUL
> (re: Noelle's text)
> Noelle says Marty Evans just broke into the house.

> CASSIE
> *Baswell's* house?

> PAUL
> (nods)
> He ran off before she could find out what he was doing but she says he looked even worse than the other day. She said he was "tripping balls."

> CASSIE
> I guess we'd better find his brother then.

Paul nods grimly. They press on.

INT. PUMPING STATION - CONTINUOUS

The door opens, letting daylight into the dark, cavernous room. Water DRIPS. A DEAD MAN lies on the wet ground, shot in the chest, clipboard pages scattered.

PAUL
What the hell happened here?

CASSIE
(fake Southern accent)
Somebody done gone Waco.

They stop again at the sound of a GIRL'S WHIMPER. Cassie puts a finger to her lips. Paul mouths "Sarah?" and Cassie nods.

The silence is broken by a CREEPY VOICE, hushed but insistent. They get running again through the winding corridor.

CREEPY VOICE
Do it! Work faster!

SARAH (O.S.)
I'm *thirsty*...!

INT. PUMPING STATION - RAW WATER RESER-VOIR - CONTINUOUS

A large round chamber, wet brick WALLS COVERED WITH IMAGES indiscernible in the dim light. A catwalk circles a deep, DARK PIT filled with water. On the stairs leading into the pit, half in and half out of the water, lies another DEAD MAN.

On the far side of the chamber, Sarah Peterson - tired, wet and messy—sits among PAINT AND SUPPLIES. She tries to paint but her arm falls limp.

CREEPY VOICE
Thirsty! *Thirsty*, she says!

The voice belongs to Hector Evans, watching from the shadows, a HUNTING RIFLE leaning against the wall beside him.

HECTOR EVANS (CONT'D)
It's a water filtration plant! Drink some and get back
to work!

She tries. Her LEG SHACKLES RATTLE, tugging at the newly fastened metal braces on the wall.

SARAH
I can't reach!

HECTOR EVANS
Fine! I'll get you some!

He picks up a metal Thermos lid, shakes dirty water out of it, and passes her on the way to the pit.

Sarah sees her chance. With her last bit of strength, she kicks a paint can directly into his path.

Hector doesn't see it roll toward him until it's too late. He trips over it, stumbles headlong toward the pit—

—and SLAMS into the railing. The cup falls, CLANGING into the deep pit until it SPLASHES into the water far below.

Hector's surprise becomes rage. WHISPERS and LAUGHTER surround him. He twitches around and around trying to locate their source. Then he focuses on Sarah, fist raised—

> HECTOR EVANS (CONT'D)
> You ungrateful little brat!

Sarah shrinks back, covering her face.

The EVIL EYES of a misshapen DARK FIGURE among her paintings glare down from the wall above her. LAUGH-ING, it WHISPERS...

Hector's eyes fall on the RIFLE. He grabs it, COCKS it—

Sarah sees and shakes her head violently.

> CASSIE (O.S.)
> *GET ON THE GROUND, HECTOR!*

Cassie stands in the doorway, weapon raised. Paul peers around from behind her.

Hector raises his hands and the rifle into the air. He slowly lowers to his knees.

Sarah pulls on her chains, weeping.

SARAH
Help me!

PAUL
You're okay now, Sarah! Everything's gonna be okay!

CASSIE
DROP THE GUN, HECTOR!

The WHISPERS and LAUGHTER taunt him. Hector squeezes his eyes shut, trying not to listen. He begins to lower the rifle, the VOICES growing in intensity, the EVIL EYES burning—

HECTOR EVANS
It's too late, Sheriff... *You. Cannot. Stop this!*

He spins the rifle, ramming the barrel up under his chin—

CASSIE
Hector, no...!

—and he PULLS THE TRIGGER.

His BRAINS PAINT THE WALL. The VOICES and LAUGHTER stop immediately.

Sarah weeps as her captor's blood sprays in her face.

Cassie approaches her, climbing down the ladder.

PAUL

It's okay, Sarah. He can't hurt you anymore.

(then)

Do you know where the key is?

SARAH

He has them. On his belt.

Cassie shines her flashlight over the walls.

CASSIE

My God... *What is all this?*

VIVID IMAGES, ARCANE SYMBOLS, and UNINTEL-
LIGIBLE WORDS cover every surface, painted by Sarah.

Paul unfastens the key ring from Hector's belt. Blood smears
on his fingers, but he appears not to notice as he brings the
keys to Sarah.

Cassie holds the flashlight beam on a painting: a caricature of
Jack Peterson smiling and holding out a hand toward them.

SARAH

That's my dad.

CASSIE

Was he here? Did you see him?

SARAH
I brought him here. He's dead, I know he was dead.
But he helped me paint. He told me stories. He kept
me safe. When they found him, Hector pushed him
into the pit.

Unlocking her, Paul reacts to this.

PAUL
You painted all of this?

SARAH
They made me.

PAUL
"They"?

CASSIE
Oh, God... *Marty*.

As Sarah gets free of her chains and hugs Paul desperately, a
CHOKED SOB comes from the doorway.
    Cassie spins on her heels, weapon raised.

MARTY EVANS
Goodness! My goodness!

Marty Evans hurries toward his dead brother.

CASSIE
Stop right there, Marty!

He falls to his knees, sobbing.

> MARTY EVANS
> Hector... Oh, sweet Hector...

Then he sees Sarah, released from her chains and hugging Paul. He looks over the walls. He stops crying. A malicious smile comes over him.

> MARTY EVANS (CONT'D)
> No matter. *It is complete.*

His gaze falls on Sarah. She shrinks back into Paul's arms.

> MARTY EVANS (CONT'D)
> Thank you, Sarah. You did extraordinary work here.
> The reward, I'm sure, will be eternal.

> CASSIE
> What work, Marty? What did you have her do here?
> Why in the hell did you two *kill all these people*?

Marty just laughs. His MANIACAL LAUGHTER ECHOES throughout the chamber, over the strange symbols and staring eyes of Sarah's paintings, over Hector's gawking corpse, and the dread-filled faces of Cassie, Sarah, and Paul.

FADE TO BLACK.

ACT FIVE

FADE IN:

EXT. DARK PINES - EVENING

The sun sets, ending another picture-perfect day in Dark Pines.

EXT. THE PETERSON HOUSE - EVENING

Through the den window, Mrs. Peterson sits at the piano, arms slack, head bowed, brooding.

She perks up at a sound from behind her. She stands, turning, and suddenly her face fills with so much joy.

Sarah runs into her arms. Het mother hugs her. They laugh and cry together, surrounded by Sarah's vibrant art.

Cassie stands in the doorway with a smile, watching them.

INT. DR. BASWELL'S KITCHEN - NIGHT

Paul and Cassie sit at the table with coffees. Cassie sips hers. Paul joins her.

CASSIE

Sarah doesn't remember anything before waking up in the treatment plant, chained to that wall.

PAUL

No confirmation for Breen's tentacles, then.

Cassie shakes her head, solemn. Paul nods.

> PAUL (CONT'D)
> It's probably for the best. I'll do what I can for him.
> We'll work through it.

> CASSIE
> So you're gonna stay in town? After all that's
> happened?

PAUL'S FLASHBACK: *In the moonlit bedroom, Alexandra looks down at his sweaty, terrified face from under the covers.*

> ALEXANDRA DARLING
> *Don't. Ever. Leave me.*

And she vanishes into the darkness.

BACK TO SCENE

Paul peers into his mug, haunted.

> PAUL
> I wouldn't feel right about leaving. At least not until
> we figure out why twenty-two innocent people were
> murdered. And what happened to Dr. Baswell.
> Noelle said Marty Evans told her "Dr. Baswell was
> right all along." I need to find out what he meant.

INT. ATTIC - NIGHT

Noelle creeps toward the opened steamer trunk.

CASSIE (V.O.)
Sarah said the Evans brothers wouldn't tell her what
they were doing out there. But Hector talked to
himself a fair bit. Something she remembered was
"we must allow passage for Its return."

PAUL (V.O.)
"Its return"? What is "it"?

Noelle moves aside knickknacks and papers, postcards and
souvenirs from exotic countries, newspaper clippings.

Her eyes alight on a LEATHER-BOUND BOOK, tied
together with twine. She picks it up and reads the hand-
written title:

SHADOW WORK:
CHRONICLING DARK PINES' PECULIAR
HISTORY OF MASS DELUSION
BY DR. T. BASWELL, PSY. D.

INT. SHERIFF'S STATION - CELLS - NIGHT

Marty Evans hums in his bunk, TEARING out faces from a
MAGAZINE.

CASSIE (V.O.)
So far, Marty hasn't said peep. I have a feeling it'll be
torture getting him to talk.

Marty blows on each disembodied face, lets each flutter to his
feet with the others. Dozens of them.

PAUL (V.O.)
He'll talk. Everyone talks. The trick is to learn how to
listen.

INT. MRS. PETERSON'S LIVING ROOM - NIGHT

On the piano, a METRONOME CLICKS. Mrs. Peterson
plays something LIGHT AND CLASSICAL.

Sarah smiles as she paints on a canvas set up beside the
piano. Too soon to tell what the image might be. Other paintings surround them. Some beautiful, some frightening.

Her ears perk up at the DOORBELL and she crosses the
room. She opens the door. Breen stands there with a hangdog
expression.

Sarah rushes out to hug him. Realizing he's been forgiven,
Breen returns the embrace. From the piano, Mrs. Peterson
smiles back at them and resumes playing.

INT. KITCHEN - NIGHT

Cassie sips her coffee, deep in thought.

CASSIE
Sarah's father coming back, the tentacles... You think
that's why the Evans brothers kidnapped her? Could
her paintings... I don't know... is it *possible*?

Paul endlessly twists the wedding band around his finger.

PAUL
Her mother said she felt like Sarah's paintings could
come alive and leap off the canvas. Did the power of
Sarah's grief literally bring a man back to life? If only
temporarily?
(beat)
Somehow I doubt that.

CASSIE
(uncertain)
Of course not.

She looks off toward the darkened window, absently
thumbing the locket strung around her neck.

Paul spots her "tell" and immediately stops twisting his ring.

CASSIE (CONT'D)
But hey, at least now we know there's nothing in the
water.

Paul grins morosely. So does Cassie. They CLINK mugs,
and each take a generous sip.

EXT. WATER TREATMENT PLANT - NIGHT

Lights from AMBULANCES, FIRE TRUCKS and SHER-
IFF'S DEPTARTMENT VEHICLES flicker over the dark
building and even darker pines surrounding it, casting long,
ghostly shadows.

EMTs, FIRE CREW and POLICE go about their business. Deputy Lawson strings police tape across the entrance. Body bags line the parking lot.

INT. PUMPING STATION - CONTINUOUS

The cavernous DRIP-DROP-DRIP of water. The evil eyes of Sarah's DARK FIGURE hold watch over the chamber.

In the pit, a GURGLE upsets the black, still water.

Then TENTACLES BURST up from the pit, flailing in the dark, and grasp at the sides as if to pull their way out...

INT. DR. BASWELL'S OFFICE - DAY

Dust-speckled light illuminates the oak and leather room, and the ANTIQUE MEDICAL ITEMS and ARTIFACTS lining the shelves.

Paul shifts in the cozy leather chair. His PATIENT, a young, morose man with movie-star good looks, sits on the sofa.

PAUL
What brought you in to see me today, Marcus?

PATIENT
Recently... I just can't stop me from trying to kill myself.

Paul tries to parse this.

PAUL
You've been acting out on suicidal thoughts?

The Patient shakes his head. He shows his WOUNDS, one by one. Slash marks on the shoulder. Gashes on the stomach. A GASH on his palm. FINGER AND THUMB PRINTS around his throat.

PAUL (CONT'D)
Marcus... those look like *defensive* wounds.

PATIENT
They are.

And the Patient looks over Paul's shoulder at the ORNATE GOLD-FRAMED MIRROR. His eyes widen as his EVIL REFLECTION swipes out at him with a knife.

The Patient scrambles back against the sofa with a YELP of fear, throwing up his arms to protect himself.

Paul turns to look at the mirror, curious. His own haggard reflection stares back at him.

Then a pale, slender hand falls on his shoulder in the mirror. He looks up and his eyes meet those of his dead wife's.

She smiles down at him. Gradually, Paul smiles back.

FADE OUT.

THE END

NOTES: This screenplay began as a novel, one of the first I'd tried writing since returning to prose from screenplays after nearly a ten-year absence.

When a few of my scripts won and/or placed in screen-writing contests, I decided to try my hand again at writing a pilot intended for TV. The rarity of a TV pilot written "on spec" (short for "speculation," the speculation being that someone in the industry might buy the script and then pony up the cash to actually produce the damn thing) getting greenlit is such that even seasoned TV writers have multiple rejected pilot scripts.

Anyway, I like the story and characters enough that I might use this as the basis of a book series someday. For now, we'll have to do with the script.

I included it in this collection as a nod to a screenplay in another horror collection, which inspired me to try my hand at writing them. The script (or "teleplay," as it's called in the book, though the term is now outdated) was Stephen King's "Sorry, Right Number" from *Nightmares & Dreamscapes*, which aired as an episode of *Tales from the Darkside*.

Reading "Sorry, Right Number" gave me the courage to try writing screenplays in a time when I'd suddenly become obsessed with the medium of film (around about when "indie" hits like *Pulp Fiction* and *Clerks* and *The Last Seduction* exploded onto the scene), and I ended up spending more than a decade working on the "craft." It's also why I now work in television, though nowhere near the creative side of the business, and why I have a decent "day job" that allow me to write these books in my spare time.

In addition to my published writing, I have adapted

several of my books into screenplays, including *Woom*, *Wild-fire*, *Ebenezer* and *The Method*. If you have any interest in the medium, you can read those scripts here. There are also many sites where produced screenplays are available. Some of my recent favorites include Eric Heisserer's adaptation of Josh Malerman's *Bird Box*, which was much different than the finished film, and Phil Hay and Matt Manfredi's *The Invitation*.

ABOUT THE AUTHOR

Duncan Ralston is the author of the horror collections GRISTLE & BONE and VIDEO NASTIES, the novellas WILDFIRE, WOOM, WHERE THE MONSTERS LIVE, SCAVENGERS and EBENEZER, and the novels SALVAGE, THE METHOD, GHOSTLAND and THE MIDWIVES.

MORE FROM SWP

For more delicious dark fiction, please visit
WWW.DUNCANRALSTON.COM AND
WWW.SHADOWWORKPUBLISHING.COM.

www.ingramcontent.com/pod-product-compliance
Ingram Content Group UK Ltd.
Pitfield, Milton Keynes, MK11 3LW, UK
UKHW022203050525
5773UKWH00004B/507